Meanwhile back at the Henhouse

ALSO BY THOMAS BLEDSOE

Dear Uncle Bramwell

Meanwhile back at the Henhouse

a novel by

Thomas Bledsoe

Alan Swallow, *Denver*

It grows harder to write, because there is much less weather than when I was a boy and practically no men and women at all.

F. Scott Fitzgerald

For Boze, because it's our first one together, a symbol of our escaping from the Country of the Blind, where Bunnyman is King.

Sex, Arthur Evans reflected, inert beside his satiate wife in the bedroom of the antiseptic colonial house on which she lavished so much passion, was not perhaps the heart of the matter, but it was at least the symbol of their regenerate compromise.

He supposed her satiate. As presumably, perhaps even unquestionably, she did him, who stretched out replete but unfulfilled alongside the woman who encompassed a life he could neither cherish nor deny.

It was midnight, and summer noises, soft and fecund, filtered up through the venetian blinds. A girl laughed somewhere in the distance, gently mocking. A car drifted by, sports car from its low roar, trailing music and soft voices. He had a cramp in his left foot.

He shifted carefully on the rumpled sheets. Vicki always fell asleep immediately after the healthy exercise they had just concluded, but she tended to be snappish when awakened. Though no one would ever guess it to look at her, relaxed and tanned and egregiously cleancut, age had not improved her nerves. These post-coital comas, as she was fond of pointing out, phrasing it more coyly if less precisely, were the only occasions on which she dozed off without the most nerve-wracking struggle. Arthur often felt like a sleeping pill, somewhat less convenient but demonstrably more effective than the variegated sedatives which jammed the small medicine cabinet Vicki had caused to be mounted in the bathroom, safely out of reach of the smaller children.

His new position achieved, he set himself to flexing his left arch until the cramp subsided. His pillow was knotted awkwardly, and he straightened it without breaking the rhythm of his therapeutic tensing. He considered lifting his butt to smooth the mattress pad, which, as usual, bunched strategically under the small of his back, but settled instead for a few ineffective wriggles. Nothing short of a complete reconstruction, he knew from old experience, would rectify things. For all her devotion to neatness, Vicki was a lousy bedmaker. Like so much of their lives, their connubial workbench boasted a trim exterior which concealed the rumpled mess beneath.

Vicki shifted slightly, farted, and lapsed into soft, flatulent snores. With a practiced hand, he tickled her just beneath the left ear, triggering her to shudder, gargle alarmingly, and resume the peaceful, faintly stertorous breathing which was the hallmark of her normal repose.

Sex. It was not that Vicki disliked it. On the contrary. She was passionate, violently, had been, to Arthur's personal knowledge, since that night, almost twenty years ago, when he had first slipped his hand beneath her dress in a parked car outside the Country Club and transformed her from a cool, well-scrubbed tennis and dance partner into the fury who had ripped open his fly and pulled him on top of her in an embrace whose violence paled all the experiences whose variety he had heretofore been rather smugly proud of.

It had married them, no doubt of that. As they lay together afterwards on the back seat of his father's Hudson, frighteningly satiate and fulfilled, he knew that something new had happened, something he must have forever. Vicki felt it too.

"That was wonderful, Art," she had said, her soul in her eyes. "Now we have to get back inside. People will be talking."

She had snapped herself back into focus, straightened her dress, and gone back to the dance as calm and poised as any respectable belle returning from a ritual bout of discriminating necking.

That should have been the tip-off, he thought, raising his foot to stroke the arch and inaugurating another series of fruitless wriggles. It was the story of their lives.

Where had it gone? Not the passion but the terror, the wonder that had wrenched him outside himself. Nowadays Vicki's ecstasy was self-contained, impersonal, as meticulously scheduled as the time clock at the Henhouse, and as healthy as calisthenics at a Girl Scout meeting. Release shone in her eyes, which were always averted, but her soul remained locked in whatever cavern it had sunk into at some point along the downward slope of their marriage.

His meditations were interrupted by a tremendous clattering, punctuated by a single despairing yowl and a hurtling of

8

bodies through the underbrush. Sophie, the Browns' cat, surprised once more at her scavenging by Oscar, the Tom from the next block. The kids had left the top off the garbage can again, and there would be the usual mess to police in the morning.

"Whuzzat?" Vicki muttered.

"Snothing," he whispered, stroking her back in the way that soothed her. "Sleep."

He lay rigid until her breathing steadied, recreating in his mind's eye the scene that had almost waked her. Oscar creeping tawny and feral across his maculate lawn, its expanse still hopelessly spotty after ten years of Vicki's unflattering comparisons to the bowling green Lambert Brown cultivated effortlessly next door, splotched with the shameful crabgrass he had glared at through endless summer dusks, phallic hose impotently in hand as the weed's hardened resistance to the latest killer mocked him. Through which Oscar, murderously lustful, had crawled noiselessly to spring on Sophie, seduced by gluttony into carelessness, and career wildly after her through Vicki's tailored shrubbery.

Arthur hoped he caught her. *As he had Vicki?*

Within a month they had been engaged, and in six they were married, settled respectably into the cottage from which they had graduated to the comfortable prison where he now lay sleepless, unmanned by memories.

"Jesus, Evans, you couldn't wait, could you?" he thought bitterly. "You had everything you wanted, you silly bastard. She didn't make you marry her."

But he knew he would do it all over again.

Nostalgia swept him back into that impassioned summer, into a landscape ravaged by time and bitterness and the need for self-justification, but still beautiful enough to fill him with a desperate loneliness for the idyll that once had been almost real.

They had been at each other from that first night, on couches, in parked cars, in the woods bordering the fairways at the Country Club, drowning in a passion which habit only intensified, to emerge clean-limbed and glowing into an intimacy which transcended the violence of their coupling. The ecstasy which joined them also served to set them apart in the quiet Southern town at which, native and stranger, they now looked with new eyes.

9

Out of a peaceful joy neither of them had expected or understood, they faced the future with a certainty they simply took for granted.

It had not been easy. The Evanses were old Phoenix family, and properly suspicious. The Ingrahams were newcomers, good blood and respectably proud. Neither cottoned, to use the language of the town's chief enterprise, to so hasty an engagement, no matter how acceptable it might be otherwise. There was no need for such indecent haste.

It wasn't easy, but it was inevitable. To give her her due, Vicki did nothing to insist on it. She accepted their union, but she made no demands; it existed, and she was content. When Arthur remarked, one night in their second week, that they had best get married, she only looked at him with her terrifying directness, said casually, "if you want," and returned to their lovemaking. In the family storms that followed, her quiet certainty carried the day when Arthur's frantic insistence would certainly have been overborne. They had decided, and that was that. They were married just before Thanksgiving. To everyone's surprise except Vicki's, there was no young Evans the following June, or for two years afterwards.

Yes, Arthur thought, Vicki had learned the facts of life. God knows where. Not, fortunately for his serenity, from any of his set in Phoenix. Her reputation, which he had borne with him into the parked car where his future was determined, was for being a cold fish; his rape was consummated before he had time to entirely readjust his views. When, some time after their marriage, he had sought to inquire about her prior experience, she had dismissed the question by pointing out that it hardly mattered now. A fact that honesty compelled him to admit. To the best of his knowledge, she had been a scrupulously faithful wife.

Where had it gone, the wonder and the terror, the intimacy that had set them apart and made them one? The hell of it was, he knew. He almost knew why, and certainly how, though nothing now told him what remained to do.

I have measured out my life in coffee spoons. It had been about like that, he thought, remembering the shock of recognition when, late as always, he had first encountered the lines in the volume of Eliot which Zelda had lent him. That was how it had gone, dripping aimlessly away into the dregs of ordinary existence until one morning he had waked to find himself married to a respectable stranger, a dutiful wife and devoted mother who shared with him only her bed, her complaints, and a joint responsibility for the façade on which she had plastered their happiness before retiring permanently to her private interests somewhere inside.

The stranger, he was now prepared to admit, that she had always been, whom only a simultaneous and limited kind of self-discovery had ever made seem more. In that bright, far country of their youth, the passion that was perhaps her sole honesty had been enough to bring them together in an isolation of fulfillment. But in the grey world adults call maturity, where sex was an accepted if somewhat grimy fact of life, it was not enough, and what had seemed fulfillment was now revealed as gratification, a lonely and distressingly unrewarding business.

The hell with it. The cramp was gone, and he stretched gratefully while preparing to purge his mind for the release of sleep. It could wait, all of it — Vicki, who knew her own way whatever caverns her soul might now be lost in; the Henhouse, where patience was institutionalized; Zelda, who made demands but had no power to enforce them; and Margie and Annie and Susie and Hank, the children who were the unwitting guardians of his ambivalent conscience.

Soon, he knew, the decision must be faced, and when it was the pillars of Arthur Evans' small world might come tumbling down around him, the shards of that seeming respectability whose rotting foundations only he could properly assay. But this night at least he would face it as he had for longer than he cared to remember, by denial and the suicidal pretense that tomorrow's eternal sameness, that infinity of dull todays, would somehow, truly and miraculously, be another day. It had happened once. Long ago. Long —

He slept. As if on schedule, Vicki's snores, nasal and querulous, rose triumphant in the darkness, plangent on the tumid Georgia night.

11

2

Night. Darkness absolute upon the primeval waters, beneath which, drifting langorously in their soft embrace, Vicki slept, serene, fulfilled, at peace. The eternal ambience flowed gently but purposefully, carrying her down, down, softly, fearlessly despite the relentless sinking, on toward something which endured beyond the blackness, the far-off good place where she was at last to be repatriated, the brightness whose first rays now glowed in the void beneath her, beacon to a Vestal queen.

No. The light moved, and revealed itself as the Enemy, hard-bright, voraciously long and threatening. It shot toward her, exposing the face she was not surprised to see was Arthur's, as it slid harmlessly along the cocoon in which she floated, self-contained and secure.

How silly he looked, she thought indifferently. He could have touched me once. Before I thought to encase myself.

He drifted past, his tail lashing impotently against the crystal ovoid, his light sucked into the blackness which again enfolded her, soft and fertilizing. The current swept her on.

Suddenly the darkness shattered. A great roar splattered brightly around her, crackling the edges of the healing night, twisting her capsule until it threatened to catapult her, half-awake and gasping in the dry air, up past the surface into the destroying light. She cringed terror-stricken, bending to grasp her knees and bury her nostrils in the fetid dampess of her hair, breathing its saving moisture until slowly the darkness returned, the angry warping subsided, and she resumed her slow, even motion through the immemorial vastness, down, down the vortex at whose extremity lay the final peace.

Peace. It soothed and encompassed her, darker than forgetfulness, stiller than loss, complete, undeniable, and almost absolute. Almost. But far beneather her, at the periphery of her impassioned blindness, non-darkness began to glow, an antinight which was not light, not the devouring sun in which, waking, she bathed herself in fruitless, self-destructive hope, but a bright, temperate radiance, the soundless echo of the fulfillment which alone made darkness irrelevant.

The glow quickened, becoming sharper and more intense, focusing at a point which, crouching in the half-sitting position that was the nearest thing to erectness her capsule would permit, she could determine was the door, half ajar, which, memory told her, led past the iron gates down the soft, treacherous slope to the round shutter that, on her signal, would flick back to implode her unerringly home.

She watched, breathless with excitement, eyes intent on the orifice which drew inexorably closer until the ovoid came to a gentle stop inches outside it, and cracked neatly open along a hitherto indistinguishable seam, from which immaculate chromium stairs dropped down to the cool surface beneath. Weak from immanence, she leaned on the arm which protruded beside the steps and lowered herself alongside the door.

It hung, impervious and glowing, the outer darkness fulfilled by the inch her predecessor, faint with happpiness, had neglected to seal. Vicki breathed the moist silence.

She was alone. With the third eye which had given her a last glimpse of Arthur's tail and now, dying, exploded into a cinerama of her dissolving cocoon, she watched the egg disappear into the nothingness with which she was surrounded. Grey peace overwhelmed her. She pushed on the door.

It swung back, spilling radiance. Inside the grotto a pink effulgence bathed her, transforming even the gate spikes with gentleness, smoothing the shadowless morass which swallowed her feet with each step, to close silently behind her as she made her way down the deceptively gentle incline. Music sounded, women's voices in a wordless but hauntingly familiar melody which rose in intensity until, as she stood at last in the level space before the great shutter, her whole being vibrated with its harmony.

She was home. *Save me,* she thought, *I submit, I submit.* She sank to her knees, her eyes fixed on the dot in the center of the aperture, which slowly, almost imperceptibly, began to open, calling her to the green coolness within. In the distance, through the liberating circle, she could see the outlines of the temple, white and silent. It was only when it was time to glide effortlessly through that she realized that she had sunk to her breasts in the ooze that was enveloping her, and understood that the scream that was beginning inside her would be buried before it could summon them, waiting assembled in the marble vault, the ceremony lacking only her climactic presence.

She waked with the scream on her lips. Arthur stirred beside her, and she patted him automatically, gentling him back to sleep. Had she dreamed? She remembered nothing, only terror and a sense of infinite loss. Whatever had awakened her, it was gone, leaving only an intense awareness of the humid, empty dark. She turned to look at the clock, glowing dimly on her bedside table. Twelve-fifteen. Damn. Damn. And she had drifted off so beautifully.

She fought wakefulness, settling herself rigidly on her side, right breast pulled carefully up, left leg extended almost to the edge of the bed, right arm cradled under the pillow, left hand at her chin. The position of sleep. The cords in her neck ached, and she pushed up the pillow until her cheek rested on the edge. Sleep, damn you, she thought, *sleep*.

Her mind raced. She felt the tension growing, the tightness beneath her skull which she would finally have to deaden, that cursed alertness that divorced her head from her sleep-hungry limbs. She felt lassitude flowing in her legs, warming her groin almost like their love-making, up into her stomach where the knots slowly loosened, freeing her body for a remembered falling, down, down into a peace which her mind, observing coldly from an infinite distance, blocked off just before the last plunge into what it told her, with desperate calmness, would be her death. Her heart skipped, and she jerked herself over on her back, breathless at her escape from what another section of her mind reminded her was nonsense. She always felt this way, and she had yet to die. But she knew, despairingly, that she could never will that last, blessed collapse into nothingness.

She would use deception. Lull it, so that somehow, at the times she could never remember even when she fed it pills, the blanket would descend on her and consciousness would lapse, naturally and evenly as it did for Arthur whenever he wished it to, and she would fall into a sleep from which she would waken as uneventfully as if it had been the most natural thing in the world. Exercise her mind. Give it a plan it would tire of. Insomnia never hurt anybody, she had read recently in

14

the *Reader's Digest*. Lying awake was almost as restful as sleep. Draw on her stores of calmness, lie there as if she expected to, as God knows she should, and at some time, when her mind and body were ready, sleep would come, the healing thief in the empty night.

She thought about tomorrow. The table was set in the breakfast room, the white dishes on the metal filigree table she had finally persuaded Arthur to buy. Mats. She hated them, but they did save ironing. Poached eggs, the stainless steel six-egg poacher already on the stove. The orange juice made in the blue plastic pitcher in the refrigerator, as Susie insisted on doing despite her warnings about what happened to the vitamins. Not that it really mattered. They all took vitamin pills, and it gave Susie a sense of responsibility. Which she could use.

Tomorrow was Katy's downstairs day. Her mind snaked through the rooms, peering in corners, straightening cushions, checking the wainscoting for dust. A quick once-over would suffice, she decided, even with her bridge lunch on Wednesday. She would get Katy after the stove. The broiler hadn't been cleaned in weeks, and there was no way to make the children wipe up after their eternal grilled cheese sandwiches. Was it inherited, she wondered, akin to the stuffed drawers, messy closets, and rumpled sheets that were her secret shame? She'd think better of Arthur if he'd only complain. She knew how he hated it. Maybe if only once he'd explode, even strike her, he would break through the wall again and touch her into life.

God damn him. God damn men, for that matter. Were there none that understood? Lambert Brown leering at her at the garden party last night, touching her breast when he leaned over to fill her glass. The damn fool. Did they all think that was the way to a woman's soul? And fuck his lawn.

Whatever made her think that? She didn't really mean it, and it wasn't like her at all. Why, I don't think I've said that word in years, she thought. If poor Arthur could hear me, after the hard time I've given him about the grass, maybe I'd break through and touch *him*. Or would I?

She giggled, and for a moment considered waking him. But she knew she wouldn't. She didn't really feel like getting all excited again, and that was the only thing they knew how to do in bed. They didn't even argue any more.

"The way to a woman's heart, my boy," she said aloud, softly but distinctly in the empty night, "is not through her cunt."

It was said, and she felt suddenly enormously pleased with herself, released by the unfamiliar vulgarity, the hard, ugly word sustaining her in the devouring loneliness. Why not? Her body was what remained to her. It was only inside that she was growing old, the juices drying deep down where only she could feel, the tight, empty shell slowly hardening beneath the soft flesh that had tempted Lambert.

No wonder they wanted her. At forty-two Arthur was already middle-aged, slim and hard and still exciting in bed, but lined and dry, his bright secret eyes peering out through a network of tiny wrinkles, hair retreating halfway back his scalp, teeth yellowed and patched with gold. Only two years older than she, and already she was beginning to look like his daughter. She only hoped her girls would stay as well-preserved.

She could feel her body in the darkness. The full breasts, still firm and assertive. Her belly flat despite the four lives it had incubated, her bush luxuriant again in the ten years since Hank had fought his way out between the thighs which now stretched slim and virginal in the fetid night.

Of course Lambert wanted her. Who wouldn't, who had drawn Lucy Brown as a bedmate, with her stringy hair, already graying, and her brittle nervous body balanced uncertainly on her pipestem legs. God. She probably talked all the time they were doing it. What would Lambert have done, she wondered, if she had led him on? Panicked, probably. There had to be something wrong with a man who grew a lawn like that. Poor Arthur.

But the gall of Lambert's thinking she'd want him. Men. Where did they get that eternal conceit, their inalienable conviction that in such an essentially simple and impersonal operation they were somehow unique? When she could tell them, any woman could. It doesn't matter that much, gentlemen. It's just not that complicated. That's why the way to a woman's heart is not. Definitely not.

There were differences in equipment. And technique. She wouldn't argue that. Arthur had been born with one and she had taught him the other. But that's where it ended. And began.

She remembered the time, early in their marriage, when he

16

had asked why she had married him. It was in the bedroom of the little house on Stonewall Street, one of the lazy Sunday afternoons they used to spend in bed, making love, reading the paper, talking about nothing and everything. He had asked her suddenly while she was studying the rotogravure section of the Atlanta *Journal,* its damp brown pages crumpled on her naked belly.

"Why did you marry me, Vicki?" he had said, dropping the sports section to look at her with eyes that were not yet veiled.

She returned the look, letting her soul speak in that time before the barrier had gone up between them, and put her hand on him, kneading and feeling it rise living in her hand until they were together in wordless joy.

The memory excited her, and she squirmed hungrily on the hot sheets. No. Think of something else. She fought her need from her mind.

Margie. She was sleeping with that Maynard boy. She'd seen it in her eyes when they came up from the rumpus room for dinner the other night. And in his pants, the erection bulging the dirty khaki slacks they all had the bad manners to wear, his empty, secretive face bland while his hand worked desperately in his pocket to conceal it. Didn't look very big, either.

Well, why not. It was the way she had started, probably the way they all must. But that didn't make it seem right. God, had they been so callow, the ones she had begun with, so unformed? Not even hungry animals, only frightened, impassive robots, their faces blank as statues, staring hopelessly with their blind eyes.

Now *she* was being foolish. God, she must be getting old. Soon she'd be as bad as Arthur, demanding something the act wasn't designed to produce. There was the trouble with men. Masterpieces of simple design, bearing between their legs the erectile tissue, immemorially Pavlovized, which rose in her service for the engulfment men called submission. Which they had to make a drama of. Give it a soul. If she weren't a lady, she'd say *shit*.

Would it have helped if Arthur understood she was an intellectual?

Certainly not. It was the *thing* that mattered, which Margie had caressed with Freddy Maynard, enveloped in the discovery

17

where her mother could no longer provide her guidance, only hope, where she someday might find the satisfying compromise which would make respectability a necessary virtue.

Which she must, she no longer denied, have again from Arthur. She touched him gently, skillfully from all the years of knowing, until the great stalk rose wildly, wakeful on its sleepy host, and she pulled him on her to lose herself in the beauty he drove savagely between her thighs.

3

What had he meant by it?

Didn't he know how she must take it? Phoenix being Phoenix and Zelda Huckaby being Zelda Huckaby, one generation removed from the Crackers Fred had transcended by sheer guts and impudence to become the protege of old Colonel Tom Carter while still maintaining residence, in the Evanses view, across the tracks in the universe from which his new house on the Macon Road had not, epistemologically, sprung him.

So.

So you didn't say *I love you* to Zelda Huckaby, not if you were Arthur Evans, unless that whole cosmos was freighted on your statement, unless you had weighed the consequences in the balance and found them not wanting. As Arthur certainly hadn't.

Damn him. To spout it so casually, not being casual at all, especially at the Henhouse, dropping it at the end of Friday's conference with Ulysses, when they were about to leave the office, turning their backs on the debris of cigarette butts and lost causes.

"Look, Zelda," he had said, his hand gentle on her shoulder as he turned to switch off the light, "I love you. Don't forget that, will you?"

Forget it? What kind of nonsense was that? How did Zelda Huckaby forget a thing like that? The only thing was, what was she supposed to remember?

Love? Love was Vicki and the children and all the Evanses and the Ingrahams, the ordained constellations of Phoenix society in which Arthur, with wrongful rightness, maintained his predestined orbit. No matter how spiritually unkempt, he would make its parades, trim and sturdy in the front rank of a company in which all his essence disbelieved. As if it mattered. Pretty is as pretty does, her father used to say. Arthur did, and it wasn't pretty. Not for Zelda. And not for him.

So what was left? Empathy, the psychologists called it.

Transference, if she erected, decidedly the wrong word, Arthur into the father image the emasculate sons of Freud aspired to. As if any child of Fred's, early or late, could bear a surrogate. That was the wrong verb too.

Communion. A dirty word, adjustment-wise, but it was what they had, maladjusted now, God knows, and unconsummated, fleshed only through books, and words, and the meaningless caresses which were the transubstantiation of a passion which surged unborn. Surged was the word.

It would *be*, damn it. He needed it as much as she, whatever the cost. How could Vicki, with her neat, antiseptic body and her chromium mind, encompass the darkness that was Arthur's light, rising from its ashes into an illumination Phoenix could not even imagine. But Zelda Huckaby could. Should. Would. *Quod erat demonstrandum.*

She rose from her chair in the severely modern compartment into which she had transformed Fred's old littered, human study. I hate it, really, she thought. It's a gesture we won't need. Then.

Then. The infinity encompassed her, and she saw it as the condominium it might become, the Spirit of Phoenix Past and Phoenix Present, enjoined through love into a Future she and Arthur were doomed to create. Capital letters, she had to admit. But Sincere.

Damn you, Zelda, she thought, that's what will do you in, that third rate pseudo-literary mind. Child of Fred's old age, suckled in the Carter Memorial Library of the War Between the States, named out of his passion for Fitzgerald, weaned at Radcliffe because Emily Carter had opted Smith, returned to Phoenix because she didn't have better sense, employed at the Henhouse because it was the only reasonably insane institution in town, unmarried by choice, in love with Arthur Evans out of proximity and, she was afraid, inevitability — how would you expect a mess like that to end up as anything but trouble? And trouble was what she had.

So she'd settle for that. Those were problems which, as Arthur was fond of pointing out in his cool, analytical way, were inherent in the situation. They were the things she could do nothing about. But there was another order of problems, the factors in any situation which exist only because of the particular people involved, which you can change by changing the individuals. The problems, in short, that she made for herself. Those were what bugged her.

Consider. She was thirty-three years old, intelligent, well educated, blessed with an independent income, reasonably good looking, and, she had it, if not from Arthur Evans at least on fairly reliable authority, an excellent lay. In love with a man who also loved her, whose susceptibility had long since passed the boiling point. Whose wife had become a total stranger. Whose job he had long since outgrown. Whose life was one big, fat, boring lie. In short, a man in a situation which was made to order for the things a woman like Zelda Huckaby aimed to do.

And what did she do about it?

Walked away from it. Kicked it around. Worst of all, gagged it up. Even when she only thought about it, she was off and running with lousy jokes like the Spirit of Phoenix Future, neutralizing herself by making it ridiculous. A girl as smart as she was could get Arthur Evans into bed, out of town, and off to a new life in six months. If she had sense enough to shut up and quit cracking wise.

All right, by God, she'd do it. Whatever Fred might think of her running off with Arthur Evans, he'd like it a hell of a lot less if he could see her glopping around without the guts to make up what passed for her mind.

"If you want him, Zel, and you're certain it's right for both of you, then go after him. At least find out where you stand. Shit or get off the pot."

That's what he'd have told her. It was what he had once said to Maud Pickett, by his own admission, in the days before Captain Tom Carter had his accident and Maud was helplessly in love with him. He'd meant it, too, even though she chose to regard it as one of his less forgivable jokes.

You can be an honest woman robbing filling stations, as long as you really believe it's all right to rob filling stations. That had been the gist of his legacy to her, and she hadn't had the motherwit to live by it. She'd inhabited his house, supplemented the respectably meager salary which the Henhouse, in its impregnable righteousness, was charitable enough to grant her, and indulged every whim her restless mind could generate. The

21

whim of an iron girl, that was her. Among whose vagaries she must now admit an implacable determination to ignore the sum of all Fred's years of passionate wisdom, the fruit of the struggle that had made him editor and sole proprietor of the Phoenix *Daily News* and had left her a silly, pampered little bitch.

Not any more, goddamn it. Arthur was no whim, and all her yesterdays were nothing to tomorrow. The only day anyone ever had was this one. Tend to it, and yesterday and tomorrow would take care of themselves. Another piece of Fred's unremembered wisdom. Jesus, it was getting to be dear old Dad night. Better have a drink on that one. He was always a quick man with a toast.

She sloshed whiskey in her glass from the half-empty bottle on the desk and sat down again, faintly unsteady in the sexless chair.

"Okay, baby," she said, "Operation Arthur is now in force. Right now. This minute. And from now on. It's official, Artie boy, as you'll damned well find out when we hit New Orleans for AAWB next week. They have beds in those hotel rooms, buddy boy, and you and Zelda are going to lay down and talk the whole thing over. And go on from there. All the way, lover. All the way. And then some."

She poured another drink, pulled over the desk chair, and put her feet on its neat Swedish upholstery. Even got striped-ass chairs in this damn house, she thought, looking up at the portrait of her father which dominated the room. Now what would Fred say to that?

Old Fred. She could imagine.

"A chair, Zelda," she could hear her father saying in his slurred, Cracker's voice, "is one of man's oldest and most honorable inventions. Antedates the wheel. One of the arts of peace. Cradle a man's ass in a comfortable chair and you've immobilized his destructive potential. Make it deep enough and you've temporarily removed him from the ranks of murderers the human race persists in regarding as its noblest creations. A man doesn't jump out of a Morris chair and make a quick draw with his sixshooter. Nossir. Man sits in a good chair and it pleasures him. For right then, anyway, that's enough."

He'd smile, flicking the ashes from his rum crook onto the old Turkey carpet that, in his time, had covered the floor for the rather considerable expanse where it wasn't worn through.

"Now that particlar chair," he'd say, bending to fill his glass and hide his self-consciousness over a pronunciation they both knew he had stolen from Colonel Tom, "I can't say it fits the specifications. It don't match my ass, or even that cute little butt of yours, Zel. I'd burn it."

And he'd be right. It was a part of the game she'd been playing, the denial of the honesty which was her birthright for the sake of the pretense which had become her goal. Thank God she was beginning to have sense enough to be ashamed of herself.

Damn right Fred was a Cracker. A Redneck. Poor white, which was what Colonel Tom had called him before he came to respect him even to the point of asking him to become his partner in the Carter Memorial Library of the War Between the States. An enterprise almost as superlatively hare-brained as the Henhouse. God, that good blood ran crazy. But better than cold.

Why had Fred succeeded? Crackers didn't become editors of sizeable Georgia newspapers, not in the old days, not even now when the myth of Southern nobility had become a camouflage for the petty resentments of that pure white miscegenation, half of them, it sometimes seemed, from Indiana, who glutted the Macon Road, the developments which aped it, and the Country Club which ingested them all.

He'd made it by guts, of course, and brains, but mainly by honesty, with himself as with others, his steadfast refusal to value himself at less than he could prove himself to be, or accord to others any consideration their performance would not justify. It was not a role that made for popularity, not at first, but it earned him respect at a time when men who could be trusted were even rarer in Phoenix than usual, and as the years wore on he accumulated the affection his sympathetic irreverence deserved. By the time of Zelda's birth he was an institution in his own right, a self-made one in a town where inheritance was still the accepted route to such eminence.

It had been an experience being Fred Huckaby's daughter, educational and demanding. At first it was all plus. The publisher of a town's sole daily newspaper is a power, and his only daughter did not hesitate to bask in his glory. Besides, Fred made it his business to know what was going on, especially if

23

it was unprintable, and Zelda, early his confidante, came into possession of certain bits of information which, with her father's sympathy if not his authorization, she did not, on occasion, hesitate to use. It did no harm to business to help spread the word that Huckabys knew the score.

Well, she learned about that bit, though it took her two grades to live down a well-deserved reputation for being a snot. Not, looking back, that the experience did her any harm. Better early than late, she had often thought at Radcliffe, hemmed in by girls who had never absorbed the simple lesson she was now certain her father had deliberately plotted. That was Fred's way. To make her find out for herself, with a little cumshaw for his own operation on the side. Too bad he hadn't figured on Arthur.

But it was only when the prom parties started, and after that the dances, that she began to realize that something else set Zelda Huckaby apart in a way no wisdom of hers, however painfully acquired, could alter. Not apart from most of the town: neither from the top, where Fred's ancient intimacy with Colonel Tom guaranteed her acceptance by the Carters, though her relationship with Emily, her contemporary, was friendly rather than warm; nor from ninety-five per cent of those whose status trailed down from that pre-eminence. Only from a small, hard core of families who, as she was happy at that time to tell herself and anyone else who cared to listen, clung to their inherited position because it was all they had left to brag about.

They spoke, pleasantly, in the same fashion that they subscribed to the *News*. But Zelda Huckaby was not invited to their parties. There was no fuss about it, no ugly words. She simply wasn't there. The Evanses were, and the Maynards, and the Wilsons, and the Shepherds, and the Ingrahams, after Vicki's clan arrived and was duly voted in. And, of course, the Carters. Above all, there were the Taliaferros, whose pride was evenly divided between a mispronunciation of their name and a rabbit-eared, sandy-haired scion named Evan.

Evan. That was a hight one. Was that unimpressive hieroglyphic to be the story of her life?

Evan Taliaferro, known as Tol to intimates who took his name less seriously than his mother, had been her sole public skirmish with that high authority which routinely defeated her by denying that any battle could exist. Tol liked her. He liked her a lot, for reasons that at this distance she still could not understand. He was an undistinguished boy, but she encouraged him, for reasons she now had no trouble being ashamed of. The summer he got his first car, he went after her hard.

Mrs. Taliaferro put a stop to that. Either Zelda Huckaby went, or the car did. No son of hers would misuse an expensive machine provided by his family in order to cultivate a relationship which common sense should have told him could lead to no good for anyone concerned.

Tol made the mistake of apologizing to Zelda. And of trying to beat the rap.

"My God, Tol," she said when he explained the dilemma, "is a car as important as all that?"

He looked at her as if she were the idiot she had just proved herself to be, and she had the grace not to persist. Tol, unfortunately, lacked the sense to stop.

"But we can still see each other, Zel," he went on. "We can each go with somebody else, see, and then we can split off and be together until it's time to go home."

"Like in the backyard behind the rosebushes?" Zelda said.

"Yeah," Tol breathed. "Like that."

They made a nondate for the Cheatham's party that Saturday, promising to arrive and depart in separate convoys, but to disaffiliate early and often. Zelda could hardly wait to pull the chain.

She took the first opportunity, when Tol came up to her for the second dance, his by prior conspiracy.

"I'm sorry, Tol," she said, with a sugary distinctness Mrs. Taliaferro herself might have envied, "but since your mother won't let you dirty your car by carrying me in it, I don't think you should sully yourself by dancing with me."

And she gave her arm to young Tom Carter, who, her name on his card, stood watching the performance with his usual amused detachment. She and Tom went a long way that evening, a bonus she had never regretted. All the destruction in him warmed to that act of calculated malice, as did his sense of justice and his contempt for Tol's smug mediocrity. But it was lonely when he dropped her at home, flushed and excited and an incalculable last step from fulfillment. It was one of the

25

few times she had genuinely regretted that her mother, freed at last she supposed, had quietly died after finally giving birth to a child. You needed a woman to share a half-triumph like that.

The price, of course, had been Tol's white-faced embarrassment, a pasty confusion illuminated only by his glowing ears. But he had survived it, moving from one car to another until the night five years later, when he had immortalized himself by smashing into a hog at seventy-five miles an hour on the open highway south of Barnesville. It had happened just this side of a culvert, into which what was left of Tol, the hog, and the car careened with such violence that the demolishment was still considered a local record.

I suppose I could have prevented it, Zelda thought, taking her feet down to ready herself for her solitary trip upstairs. He sure as hell couldn't have done it if the old bag had taken his cars away. I wonder if she ever thought of that.

Perhaps she had, though Zelda suspected that, beyond relief, Mrs. T's reaction to her performance with Tol had been a mixture of reluctant admiration and regret that a girl who could carry that off was stigmatized by hopelessly bad blood. Maybe Mr. Taliaferro thought about it too, in the last microseconds of his own private aftermath. Superficially, he had carried on as usual after his son's death, performing his meager duties at the Henhouse and his other civic and social responsibilities, including the consumption of a quart of good bourbon a day, with his accustomed gentle confusion. But a few months after Tol's holocaust he began to suffer from the incurable rash of boils which became the direct cause of his own end.

My God, Zelda thought, beginning to move unsteadily up the stair, I could have saved Arthur too. She had never put it to herself just like that before, but what she had done was clean out the whole damned succession. Harry Taliaferro, son of the founder of the Taliaferro Institute for the Blind, locally known as the Henhouse, bore his affliction with his habitual gentleness, but he did take certain steps to minimize the inconvenience. Among these was neglecting to look up and down the tracks alongside the Henhouse when he knew no train was scheduled, an accommodation to his tortured neck which brought him, one morning her last year at Radcliffe, ungently in front of the eight-fifteen, roaring out of Phoenix forty-five minutes late.

26

Becoming instantaneously, in an immolation which rivaled his son's, past President and General Manager of the Taliaferro Institute, where he was succeeded, first as Manager and subsequently as President, by his capable and eminently respectable assistant, Arthur Walker Evans, who assumed his new duties, with the distraught widow's fulsome approval, one month before Zelda Huckaby's graduation and seven years after his marriage to Vicki.

4

The Henhouse.

Now there, Captain Tom reflected, erect in the wheelchair which cradled his shattered spine, was a name of which Phoenix could be justly proud, a triumph of the folk mind over the caste system into which he had been born unasked. Phoenix wasn't, of course. The name was merely taken for granted, its rebellious edges blunted, its fine country fragrance filtered through the odorless commonplace. Gone the way of all phrases that once had meant something. Like drunk as a judge.

Well, he wasn't that yet, though he would be. Meanwhile, the evening was young. S. T. had just rolled him up to his room, settled his glass in the rack, and placed the bottle conveniently beside the chair. Essie's dinner still worked inside him, warm and deceptively sobering. It was his favorite time of day, better even than the hour after breakfast. Delicately poised between the day's vague drabness and the night's oblivion, he had escaped to a plateau of joyous clarity, from which he could survey the small universe in which he was forever condemned to be a spectator, and render the judgments in which his freedom was still unimpaired.

Judge. Had Phoenix ever had a sober one? Certainly not old Virginius Taliaferro, father to Harry and grandsire to Tol, a drunkenly arrogant man whose line had ended abruptly in the automobiles he hated.

The judge was a horse and buggy man. A horse man, to be precise, born into a time and place where the automobile and the mule would exterminate the breed he loved. Well, the Captain could understand that. He was a horse man too. Had been, that is, before a striker's bullet from the darkness had crumpled him on the steps of the meeting where he had gone once more, however vainly and ambivalently, to plead their cause. God, how they'd hated him. A feeling he reciprocated.

How long now? 1930, twenty-three years. What he missed

most, if anyone should ask him, as no one would, were horses and walking. It might have been women, had Margaret not subsided so early into indifference. But she was no loss, now that his body was gone, and those he'd had in his mind were still his. Available.

Lords. They were the drunk ones, weren't they? Judges were sober. Like hell they were. No more than he. But it was walking he was thinking about.

God, it had been wonderful. To stride along in a clean white linen suit, feeling his hips articulate, swinging his weight forward as the muscles of his buttocks and belly began the proud thrust of knee and thigh, down the taut calf to the waiting foot, which arched from heel to toe to catapault him into another cycle. All dead now. But alive then, flexing and tensing in a rhythm that was an ecstasy of pure motion.

Horses were even better. The broad back warm and living beneath him, the whole animal an extension of his own body, which adjusted effortlessly to otherbody's movements, guiding with his knees and hands, master but partner, always conscious of union with another life. On horseback he was more than a man, a communicant in a symbiosis which gave life a new dimension. If centaurs had not existed, the mythological mind would have been forced to invent them.

Idle thoughts. Dangerous. More of that and he'd end up like poor old Bramwell Wilson, only he'd have to get S. T. to roll him out under a tree first. The paradox freed him, a vision of S. T., cat-black and elegant, wheeling him carefully out to the spot where he was to pop down his cyanide, making certain everything was in order, the capsules at hand on the bourbon-stained rack he had created, before leaving him to complete the ritual. S. T. would do it, too, the Captain thought affectionately. By God he would.

But how did he let himself get here, after all his years of discipline?

The Henhouse. And Judge Virginius Taliaferro. The drunken old sonofabitch.

Now there was a man with discipline, in everything except the bottle. Take the way he started the Henhouse. When a man's beautiful young wife is permanently blinded by being jerked out of a buggy and dragged by a horse everyone else knows is too much for her but he insists she drive because it's sporting — after that, you'd think a man's passion for the beasts might cool. But not the Judge's. He waited on her, whom he apparently loved as much as could anyone, for the rest of her life; founded the Taliaferro Institute for the Blind out of guilt and as a place to keep her busy; and devoted himself to promoting it even after she was dead. But he never changed his tastes. He even kept the horse that blinded her.

It didn't stay the Taliaferro Institute long. Not in Phoenix, anyway. From the beginning, the Judge, a shrewd businessman even when endowing a charitable enterprise, employed only women because they would work for nothing, or close to it, for so worthy a cause. The same way, come to think of it, that Fred Huckaby, a few years earlier, had hired Maud Pickett for the Library. The town, amused by the little hive of female agitation Virginius presided over, but also rebelling, the Captain felt certain, at the misspelling of Tolliver, perhaps at the mispronunciation of Taliaferro, which was generally considered stuck-up, christened it the Henhouse.

Which it remained. As had its policies. To this day they had only two men, Arthur Evans and Ulysses Futral. They must have a boy someplace back in the shipping department, but women even assembled the damned machines. All the others, Zelda Huckaby —

So that's where all this was taking him. He might have known.

Was he really so frightened about Emily that it took him this long, over such a devious route, to get to Zelda and the immediate problem? If he was, and he might be crippled but he wasn't stupid enough to deny that this was the essential truth, then he also could afford to endure a while, as absolutes deserved, and postpone the pragmatic decision. If, that is, he could also postpone oblivion.

Let's see. He'd had two, no three, since S. T. wheeled him in. It took at last six to push him past the edge. He poured another drink. There was time.

The greatest sorrow of his unmaimed life had been that Emily and Zelda were not closer. Child of his youth and fruit of Fred's ancient loins, these unpremeditated beautiful daughters had been the chance, heaven-sent to a pair of unregenerate

30

atheists, to consummate the union which Maud Pickett had only improbably symbolized. Maud, their partner at the Carter Memorial Library of the War Between the States, was the chronological median between their generations, and she had loved him as, in her way, he had her. But her way did not embody the passion of his life, and he had not the wisdom, nor she the imagination, to achieve a synthesis. The irony, which neither of them could prophesy, was that Maud would have been better in bed than Margaret. And a better heitage for Emily. Checkmate.

Zelda and Emily arrived unprogrammed but beautiful, obviously procreated to bridge the gap between Fred, who was Old Tom's generation, and Captain Tom, who was Fred's spiritual son. As they grew up, bright and lovely and rebellious, the girls' affinity became increasingly clear. To everyone except themselves.

Which was how it stayed. Emily and Zelda never had a harsh word or, to the Captain's knowledge, an intimate moment. Their patterns were almost identical. They were valedictorians in succeeding years and migrated to cousinly Eastern women's colleges, Zelda having made the prior departure but Emily, as the Captain discovered during the family crisis that preceded her leaving, the chromosonic decision. But from then on the genes took over.

Emily married one. Gene Alexander, painter, life force, blood brother, however excommunicate, to the Captain, who had loved him even at the ceremony at which he blessed his daughter out of his life. Gene had become, as any intelligent invalid could predict, the man under whom she was destroying herself through her inability to understand. Or control.

Recklessly, he poured another drink. Easy, Tom, he cautioned himself while he gulped it, there was something you had to decide. As if it mattered. Emily had made the decision, which he supported, not to come home. It should have been right for her, he had reasoned, remembering that he had come back and it had been wrong for him. And her. So she had gone, to the chance he had never had with Margaret, and now would die. The hell of it was, down deep or up high, it didn't matter which, he sympathized with Gene.

He put his drink on the rack and forced himself back to Zelda.

She'd done the opposite. She'd come home when she knew better and stayed when she found worse. And now must face the same decision. And he had to speak.

As who? Father, through Fred? Brother, through Emily? Lover, through Arthur? Group Conscience, as homeopathic witness to an ingrown community? Or Prophet, as the emasculate symbol of a dying world?

Suppose they all said the same? And suppose this was the one message Zelda could not afford to hear? As it had to be. And it was.

Death. They'd kill her if she kept on. One way or another.

I hate the goddamned drama, his mind said while his heart panicked and his hand snaked out and captured the bottle. Despairingly, he buried its neck in his mouth, swallowed, and slid off the plateau into oblivion.

While her elders stumbled through the wreckage they had made of their lives, Margie Evans slept dreamless and fufilled. Her face, a feminine replica of Arthur's aquiline features, was rosy with heat, the lip above her opened mouth dewy with perspiration. In any light, she would have been innocence made visible; in the darkness, her even breathing was a symbol of peace.

As usual, the darkness was right. Innocent Margie was not, through the peace of ignorance was still hers. But inside that soft, faintly pudgy body, whose full curves so excited Freddy Maynard but which her mother warned her could quickly run to fat, a seed was growing, a microscopic egg without soul, identity, or sex, which differed from the multitudes her ovaries routinely spawned only in one tiny particular. It was newly fertilized.

That afternoon, to be precise, when, on the back seat of Freddy's car parked on a familiar sideroad off the Newnan highway, they did what they had now done often enough to be careless. She had balked at first, since Freddy had no preparations.

"Aw, come on, baby," he whispered, his hand alive in her crotch, his manhood urgent to her touch, "we gotta. It'll be all right. You're about to fall off the roof anyway, ain't you?"

It was true, almost, and she abandoned all resistance, wanting it as much as he, the hot spasm whose joy she had inherited from Vicki, the fierce thrust which drove her outside herself, beyond Freddy's awkward ignorance to a flowering from which she returned only slowly to consider what she had done.

"Gee, I hope it's all right," she said when she began to realize how uncomfortable she was. "Move some, honey. Not using anything, I mean."

"Sure it is, Margie," he said, fear prickling him now that desire was gone. "It's only a couple of days. It must be started already."

She let herself be convinced, believing it anyway since she knew nothing could happen this close, and when she drifted off to sleep that night, she had nearly forgotten it.

She had been almost right. Another day, and the immemorial cleansing would have begun, the first trickle of the flood whose absorption, concealment, and deodorizing support a substantial segment of the American economy. Instead, while Margie slept peacefully, on the night when Arthur, Vicki, Zelda, and the Captain wrestled with their souls, new life had been created, a speck which would magnify with terrifying rapidity, to become at last the decisive factor in the tragedy which would overwhelm them all.

To reach the Henhouse you drove north from the Monument, turning right off Court Street, if you were a native, along the dirt road that curved through the colored section. Hardly the scenic route, Arthur thought as he wound along past the grey board shacks with their swept clay yards. God knows why he still took it. It was dusty, unlovely, and saved perhaps a quarter of a mile. But the old-timers always went that way when it wasn't raining, and Arthur Evans knew which side his ruts were unpaved on. Yes, indeed.

Like hell he did.

Why did he always have to torture himself? The real reason, and he knew it, was that it was almost the only place left in town where he could recapture a fragment of the illusion of his youth, tooling along in the old Hudson on the clay roads that snaked out through the red countryside, past cotton fields, sorghum patches, and an occasional country store, its weathered sides patched with the Bull Durham and Black Jack signs that were its most durable parts. The route he and Vicki had traveled in the lost past.

Last night returned to him, waking again in the act of love, meeting Vicki's passion with the violent tenderness of their beginnings, repatriated, as it were, to the back seat of a car parked along the roads where his mind now wandered, all of him poured into her so intensely that only afterwards did he realize from her silence that he had once again been alone.

Damn. He'd run through the stop sign at end of the cut-off again, narrowly missing a pick-up that crossed the tracks where the highway bent north toward Atlanta. God, he must be getting old. A few more like that and the Henhouse would have another Past President, dispatched in a distressingly similar fashion. He wondered what old Harry had been thinking about when he rode onto that track. Probably the drink he'd have at the office he never reached.

He was driving out past the Experiment Station now, slowing instinctively to cross the spur line that came in from the west. Automatically, his eye caught the tree under which they'd found Bramwell Wilson, and he shuddered. Poor bastard. A hell of a way to die. Cianide before breakfast. No breakfast ever. Harry had it better than that.

Enough of that, Evans, he told himself. That's no answer. Guiltily, and with a tinge of fear, he realized that his genuflection at the spot of Bramwell's suicide was becoming a ritual. No matter how many stop signs he might abstractedly run, he never missed looking up when he passed the tree, even craning his neck on the ride back to catch it on the rise from the crossing, behind the privet hedge where he could glimpse it briefly before it fell behind.

An obsession. He remembered the look Zelda had given him Friday, his gaze returning after its compulsive infidelity to intercept her appraising glance with no understanding but with an instinctive guilt that puzzled him. Why that look and why does it bother me, he had thought with a corner of his mind that was not occupied with her precise analysis of the afternoon's crisis. She had not paused in her dissection, nor had she commented afterwards, an uncharacteristic bit of reticence which should have been enough to send his mind scurrying back along its tether to the ravel he had ignored. But he had forgotten. Only now, for no reason, had he abruptly realized that his habit of looking at Bramwell's tree had become obvious to her long before he had even begun to understand that it was a habit.

And to who else, he thought in sudden panic. With Zelda his defenses were down, irretrievably no matter how careful he might have been to deny it, especially to her. Deny it by touching her, however lightly, minutes before they passed the tree, when he had told her for the first time that he loved her. Which was hardly the point right now.

Oh Jesus, he thought, couldn't he keep his thoughts straight for two seconds running? What had become of the calm rationality he had built his reputation on, the cool, analytical manner about which Zelda loved to twit him? Her long flank firm and warm within the full skirts under which she would tuck her brown calves, burying her toes sensually somewhere beneath her. Her trim breasts swelling the tailored white blouse, one lean, intelligent hand cupping her square chin while the other

36

lay alertly idle in her lap. Bringing life to the seat that now stretched empty beside him, dispassionately analyzing Ulysses' objections while her whole body spoke of love.

Goddamn it. He forced his mind back to the road and realized he had overshot the turnoff to the Henhouse. One of these days he *would* kill himself. How long had he been wandering in the fog that enwrapped him every time his mind raced? Weeks? Months? An eternity. Maybe it was physical. His whole body was clouded too, as if his pores were stifled. His hands tingled, and he had trouble breathing. And that invisible clamp on his head, tightening until his ears rang. He must be rundown. Which was why he'd played three sets Saturday and hardly gotten winded. And felt marvelous bright clarity until he turned in the driveway at home.

But his body was involved. Passionately. Why didn't the books on logic talk about that, give him a way back to the simple paths he knew so well? How did you think when the red mist descended, when your whole being was in a state of funk? He ought to read Scott Fitzgerald's *The Crack-Up*. A damned wonder Zelda hadn't given it to him before.

He turned at the next cross-over and pulled off the side of the road. All right now, Evans, he told himself, let's think this through. Forget Zelda. Ulysses we'll deal with at the office. The question is whether anybody else has noticed that revealing little obsession with the oak tree, the gesture that could clue them to your panic. The answer is *no*. Vicki hasn't ridden that way with you in months, and no one else but Zelda has come often enough or would notice if they had. Your front's all right, buddy. And God knows you need it, considering the mess inside.

Briefly secure, he lit a cigarette and permitted himself to wonder how he had allowed desperation to encircle all his defenses. For what now seemed a lost eternity he had been the Arthur Evans people almost knew, mildly discontented like any intelligent husband, something of a fraud but sufficiently happy in his work and certain in his competence, adequately rewarded in status and dignity, debt free, living a life comfortably this side of quiet desperation. And then, one day like any other, it had all changed. Vicki had become unbearable and Zelda irresistable; his children, hitherto undistinguished but comfortable, began giving him fits; his sinecure at the Henhouse proliferated crises; and he, solid, reliable, and anything but self-destructive, had taken to gawking longingly at the spot where Bramwell Wilson had shuffled off his mortal coil in a thoroughly unamiable fashion.

It was nonsense. He had no intention of dying, and he knew it. Unless he managed to kill himself by mooning along in his car, which was becoming unpleasantly likely, he had more years ahead of him than at the moment he had any use for. His problems at the Henhouse could be settled in a week if he would only put his mind to it. Suppose he lost. Nothing had changed the essential relationships, and he had endured these comfortably for seventeen years. The kids were only normally obstreperous. They were probably no different than in years past, and it was only his irritability that magnified small matters into calamities. As for Zelda, they could begin an affair tomorrow. With all the opportunities work and travel provided them, the odds were that Vicki would never hear of it. Even if she did, there was damned little she could do about it. And an equal probability that she wouldn't care.

It was beautiful — logical, water-tight, and utterly useless. It wasn't the logical surface of his mind that was obsessed with Bramwell Wilson. Down deep where the primeval tides surged, in the impenetrable blackness of his final self, the dark gods had wakened and were displeased. Doom ringed him. On every side the enemy waited, relentless and implacable. He was afraid.

He looked at the hand that held the cigarette, the long fingers beginning to yellow from the excess smoking even Vicki had commented on, the blue veins moulded against the firm skin. It was a good hand, a fit companion for Zelda's lean grasp, a stranger to Vicki's stubby paw.

He took a deep breath and flicked the cigarette out the window. So be it. It was the irresolution that was killing him. Either he moved, or Bramwell's way would come to seem the only one. That much logic remained to him, and a knowledge of how he must go. Zelda. There was no other answer. Which meant perhaps that there was none at all, but at least he would no longer be alone, and whatever happened, they would not strike him down with his own hand.

He reached instinctively for a cigarette, realized it, and

shoved the pack back into his pocket. The hell with that. For the first time in months he felt free, and he was damned if he'd celebrate with the symbol of his harrassment. His favorite pipes still cluttered the rack on the corner of his desk, alongside the humidor whose untouched tobacco the maid freshened regularly with a bit of apple. How long since he'd smoked one? And how much longer since the peaceful days when a cigarette had been a rarity?

Well, he could change that. Smiling, he put the car into gear, turned carefully around, and headed back toward the Henhouse.

7

The Taliaferro Institute for the Blind was conceived in guilt and splendid irrationality; that it ever became more than a blind woman's plaything was due only to its founder's arrogance and his implacable determination to get his money's worth.

Judge Virginius Taliaferro knew nothing of the blind. And cared less, save only for Bessie Taliaferro, whose dead eyes haunted him past the bourbon with which he was accustomed to ward off all unpleasantness. She never reproached him, which made it worse. The unbearable fact was that he could see her, mild, self-contained, and still beautiful, knitting quietly in the rocker he had bought the year after their marriage, enduring the meager recreation left to her while he took on his usual forage before dinner.

The Institute was born on such an evening.

"Virginius," she said, startling him from a guilty reverie.

"Yes, Bessie."

"If only we could do something."

"Do something, Bessie?"

"Yes. Something that would bring good out of it."

"Good out of what, Bessie?" he said, immediately regretting the truth his lie would evoke.

"My blindness, Virginius. I think about it, sitting here in the dark, and I know God must have a reason. He must have meant something to come from it, Virginius, something we haven't found yet that He's waiting for us to do. Something that would bring happiness to others, something I had to find darkness to understand."

"Would you be happier then, Bessie?"

"I would be happier, Virginius, because it would be God's will."

"All right, Bessie," he said, not bothering to wipe the tears she could not see, "if you want it, it's there, and we'll find it. I don't know what it is, but we'll find it."

"God wants it, Virginius. He will guide us."

The Judge went to bed drunk that night, but next morning at ten he was waiting in Colonel Tom Carter's office, sober and purposeful.

"If it ain't the Judge," the Colonel said when he sauntered in at ten-thirty, immaculate in his eternal white linen suit, black string tie, and soft Panama. "What brings you here this time of morning, Virginius? Can't be anything good this early."

"A little personal business, Tom," the Judge said, rising heavily from the hard oak bench he'd been dozing on. "Need some advice. Got a minute?"

"All day for you, Judge," the Colonel said, taking him by the arm and ushering him into the inner office. "No callers, Ora Lee. The Judge and I are in conference."

He closed the door, hung his Panama carefully on the hatrack, and seated himself in front of his roll-top desk.

"Cheroot, Virginius?" he said, biting the cigar he had chosen with ritual care and splatting the end neatly into the spitoon.

"Little eye-opener, maybe?" the Colonel said when the rich smoke wreathed them. "Business'll keep that long, I reckon."

"Reckon it will."

The Colonel extracted a bottle and two glasses from the bottom of the desk, poured them half full of Bourbon, and passed one to the Judge.

"Another day," he said, lifting his glass. "I can't say I've deserved it, but I'm sure as hell going to enjoy it. Your health, Virginius."

"Yours, Tom. At least we can see."

"So it's Bessie," the Colonel said, tilting back to blow smoke at the ceiling. "She ailing?"

"She's fine. But she wants something."

"Something I can help you give her?"

"She don't know what she wants. That's what I want to talk to you about."

"Then suppose you tell me about it."

While the Judge talked, the Colonel smoked quietly, occasionally interrupting his meditative puffs to admire the lengthening ash.

"It's been my experience," he said when the Judge had finished, "that the good Lord does his best work when he's got a couple of sinners helping him. I reckon we qualify for that, Virginius. But why'd you come to me? Bessie's the only blind woman I ever knew."

"You're the fellow thinks things up around here, Colonel, and I need some thinking up. Like the Monument. Or that Library I hear you been talking to Fred Huckaby about."

"That got around already?"

"Things do," the Judge said as his ash fell off.

"Good inch and a half," the Colonel said. "Not bad. Ought to be something public, you think?"

"How I figure it."

"How about an Institute? Nice sounding kind of name. Seen a bit of them, traveling around for the Monument."

"What kind of Institute?"

"Got to *have* it, Virginius, before you can figure out what kind it is. Need a name first. Something like the Phoenix Institute for the Blind."

"Taliaferro Institute for the Blind. Sounds like a school."

"Don't have to."

"Then what would it do?"

"Can't tell you that, Judge," the Colonel said, dropping his ash gently into the tray a microsecond before it would have fallen, "but I know where to find out."

Thus birthed, the Institute quickened under the Judge's exasperate hand. A visit to the Georgia Academy for the Blind in Macon, the Colonel's first suggestion, led to nothing more than a pleasant morning, a good lunch, and the polite implication that, much as Judge Taliaferro's well-meaning interest was appreciated, the School had Georgia's problems well in hand. The Judge drove home in a fury, arriving with his horses lathered in sweat, and only the sight of Bessie's expectant face and empty eyes saved the project from immediate abandonment.

But at the American Printing House for the Blind in Louisville he found his answer. B. B. Huntoon, the energetic and imaginative Superintendent of the Printing House and of the Kentucky Institute for the Blind, listened attentively, in his office in the handsome domed building on Frankfort Avenue, while the Judge explained his nebulous mission.

"Mind if I speak frankly, Judge Taliaferro?" he said in his high voice.

"Not at all," the Judge said, suspecting that he might mind

42

a great deal but preferring it, on the whole, to the genteel brush-off he'd received in Macon.

"All right. From what you tell me, you've got no idea what you want. Your wife got blinded in an accident you feel guilty about, and now she wants to do something that'll make her feel there's some good in it. You're willing to humor her if you can figure out something that doesn't cost too much. That about right?"

The Judge reddened, half rose, and then sank back into his chair.

"That's it," he said levelly, recognizing a man he could do business with.

"You're a good man, Judge," Huntoon said, his lean body suddenly relaxed. "I thought you'd blow up and leave when I gave it to you straight. That's what amateurs usually do. But you took it instead of hating me. I can help you."

"I didn't come here to like you," the Judge said. "I came to find out what I could do with my Institute."

"All right, we can play it that way too. I suppose Mr. Williams gave you the tour down at Macon."

"He did. That and a lot of hot air."

"A characteristic of our profession, I'm afraid. We don't get many tough-minded ones. However. You saw the children and got a sense of the problems he faces, the same ones we have here at the Institute. And I suspect he told you this was it."

"That's right. He did."

"But it isn't, Judge. It isn't even the beginning. Or rather, it's only the beginning. Listen to me. I wear two hats, one at the Institute and one at the Printing House. Don't think I underestimate education, Judge, I've spent my life at it, but for me there's no doubt which is most important. The Printing House, much as it might pain some of my colleagues to hear me say it. And it's really only started. Fourteen years ago the Congress passed an Act to Promote the Education of the Blind and set us to administer the funds. Made us textbook printers for the schools for the blind and put up cash to pay for the books. A great mission, Judge Taliaferro, and a great responsibility, but it only scratches the surface. Do you understand?"

"I don't understand what this has to do with me."

"Everything, Judge. Everything. What the Printing House

43

does for these children is to give them sight, in a way. We're giving them something to read, the tools for their education. But only the children, and the great majority of blind people are not children. They're adults like your wife, older people mostly who've lost their sight either through accidents or natural causes. What do we do for them? Too often we give them brooms to make or baskets, if they need trades, or busy work if they don't. But their minds, man, that's where the hunger is, that's the need. That's what your Institute can do something about."

"Print books for them, you mean? I don't know as I could finance a thing like that."

"But you can, Judge. You can start small, even stay that way if you like. One font and one press, and you can do things you never dreamed of. This thing's only started, I tell you, we're still arguing about what system to use. There's a fight you can get in on will influence the education of the blind for the next hundred years. You do what I tell you, Judge, and the Taliaferro Institute for the Blind will be more important than anything your wife has even imagined. And for a modest investment. Come on. Let me show you our shop."

The fruit of Huntoon's canny idealism, distilled in the Judge's rigid practicality, produced a spirit of unexpected potency. In spite of himself, the old egotist was trapped in an enterprise irretrievably benevolent. Applying the same ruthless business sense that had made him Phoenix's first textile king, he began with the relation of customer and product, and thus bypassed the profound emotional commitments in which progress was mired. When Huntoon described the advantages of dot printing over fine letter, climaxing his exposition with a demonstration by a blind girl whose intelligent fingers read both, the judge had no doubt that, no matter how much tradition might sanction the embossed Roman letter, his money would go on the dots. But in Huntoon's subsequent impassioned defense of New York Point against the pretensions of Braille he sensed the enthusiast, and his mind raised the warning signals which had averted many a business disaster.

He thanked his host, almost politely, and headed straight for Jacksonville, for a visit with Frank H. Hall, Superintendent of the Illinois Institution for the Education of the Blind, whom

44

Huntoon described as an energetic newcomer whose inexperience made him an easy mark for the schemers in the Braille camp. The Judge found Hall not only energetic but inventive, and he left Jacksonville, averting his eyes from the Yankee monument that graced its Square, with a promise that one of the new stereographing machines, which the Superintendent was developing to supersede the cumbersome hand-set type employed at the Printing House, would find its way to the Taliaferro Institute for the Blind. Hall kept his word. By 1900, when the American Printing House for the Blind, having had Braille rammed down its throat as a climax to years of internecine warfare among the Superintendents, finally permitted stereograph machines within its portals, blind adults throughout the South had for almost five years been enjoying Braille literature from the press of the Taliaferro Institute for the Blind.

Thus the Henhouse began a tradition of service as a result of its founder's absolute indifference to it. For the Judge it was another business, non-profit and charitable, but a business nonetheless. The blind were his customers, and they would damn well use his products. Bessie, who was immediately plunged into an intensive course in Braille, became an itinerant teacher, riding a circuit of benevolence to drum up trade for the factory back in Phoenix. A room in the Henhouse, which the Judge began constructing that fall, was set aside for classes, and their first publication, prepared with the assistance of Mr. Hall, was a mail order course in Braille.

With his customary thrift and indelicacy, the Judge located the Institute, not in an elegant wing such as Colonel Carter would add to his house for the Carter Memorial Library of the War Between the States, but in a plain, square building constructed on a plot adjoining one of his cotton mills. Thus unfashionably situated, it enjoyed the practical advantages of easy accessibility for all forms of shipment and delivery, and a psychological boost for its image as a place where work got done. Another example of the way the Judge's prejudices turned to gold, like the final fillip in his decision to adopt Braille, which was not Mr. Hall's common sense nor the monomania of New York Point's developer, Mr. William Wait, but the plain fact that Wait, the Superintendent of the New York Institute for the Blind, was a unreconstructed Yankee.

45

The Henhouse acquired its name that first year as well. In defiance of all tradition but in deference to economy, the Judge trained women as typesetters and binders, and as operators of his new stereograph machine and press. Except for one Negro to manhandle shipments, there was not another male in the place until 1915, five years after Bessie's death, when the future walked in the door in the person of Ulysses Futral, a gangling eighteen-year-old with a grade school education and a passion for machinery.

He came opportunely. Twenty years service had developed erratic habits in the original equipment, and even the new machinery, purchased only five years before, was displaying signs of sympthetic unreliability. The maintenance man borrowed from the mill was beginning to mutter alarmingly about replacements and to find excuses to busy himself on a loom whenever breakdowns at the Henhouse occurred. When Ulysses appeared, ready and eager to work, practically for nothing if he were given a free hand with the machinery, the Judge was willing to ignore his sex and hire him on these terms.

Things picked up after that. Within two months the equipment was operating with its primal efficiency, and before a year was out both the stereotyping machines and the presses blossomed forth with the first of the modifications which flowered unceasingly in Futral's inventive mind. Even in that first year, as the event later proved, he had already conceived the device that was to transform the Institute.

The Judge saw it first one afternoon in 1918, when he surprised Ulysses at his bench in the corner of the pressroom, busy at a curiously shaped instrument with six familiar but oddly placed keys.

"What's that, Ulysses?" he asked, peering over his shoulder.

"Why, Judge," Futral said, obviously embarrassed, "I didn't know you was here."

"Just wandering, Ulysses," the Judge said. "What're you doing?"

"Just fiddlin, Judge."

"What's that?"

"Just a thing I been playin with. It don't work yet."

"That a braillewriter?"

"Kind of, Judge. It's just an idee."

"That's not a Hall, is it?"

"No, Judge," Futral said, satisfaction creeping into his voice, "it ain't a Hall. It's sort of my own design."

"Let's see that thing, Ulysses. Where's the carriage?"

"It don't have one, Judge," Ulysses said, his pride unleashed at last. "Here, let me show you. These things here, see, they come up one after another when you press the keys down and they emboss the cells in order. Only it don't quite work yet. But it will."

It did, too, even though it took Ulysses three years more to perfect it, and when it did the Henhouse was off and running in a new endeavor. In a field where new ideas were accustomed to languish in a morass of passionate complacency, the Taliaferro Braillewriter was an immediate success. It was simple and efficient, it was fast and easy to operate, and, as Ulysses made certain, it was available on demand. It had only one flaw, which no one could have foreseen as tragic. It was fragile.

Fragile, that is, within the context of the abuse to which it would inevitably be subjected. Ulysses Futral was a conscientious workman, and he had created his love child to withstand the shocks and hazards of everyday existence. But he had no way of knowing the habits of those whom his device would serve — neither the aggressive roughness of blind children, since he had never in his life set foot within their schools, nor the occasional awkwardness of the sightless adult, since Bessie was the only blind human whom the Judge, a segregationist here as elsewhere, had condescended to make a member of his labor force. So Ulysses constructed a machine which, handled with care, would last for decades. And which broke every time it was dropped.

An arrangement which could hardly be improved on, it seemed to the Judge, who went to his grave believing that the repairs which kept Ulysses gainfully employed in his cubicle off the pressroom were a dividend granted by a judicious God to the Taliaferro Institute as a reward for its diligence and enterprise. Even after his death in 1925 and the elevation of his son Harry to the Presidency of the Henhouse, events seemed to prove the wisdom of this judgment. An even balance between assembly and reconstruction was maintained, the girls worked up to but not beyond their capacity, and Ulysses found time

47

both to make all repairs and to perform the final adjustments without which he would not permit any new writer to leave the shop. All was right with the world.

Except that the Judge, only quasi-omnipotent despite his fearsome certainty, had overlooked a thing or two.

One was the rigidity of Ulysses' habits. Another was a paradox of the sort which the Deity on whom he depended had a weakness for committing—the onset of retrolental fibroplasis, infant blindness resulting from the oxygen therapy employed to save the lives of premature children, which, in the decade before its cause was tracked down, enormously increased the incidence of blindness and the potential demand for Taliaferro Brallewriters. The last, and most important, was the growing power and continued ignorance of his Board of Directors.

There had been a Board from the beginning, with Colonel Tom Carter as Chairman and half a dozen other solid citizens rounding out its membership. During the Judge's lifetime the Board was no more than a legal formality, rubber-stamping his decisions and approving his annual report over a sociable glass or three. Even with young Harry's accession, it continued to play its pro forma role, giving advice when it was solicited and assuming responsibility for the first time only when Harry, rebelling against a position which actually required him to work, demanded the employment of an assistant who could free him for more congenial pursuits. The Board listened and took action, hired Arthur Evans and, in so doing, assumed direct control of the Henhouse. Its grip tightened when Arthur became Manager. By the time of his election to the Presidency, the Board was in no mood to relinquish its power, a fact that was demonstrated to him, pleasantly but firmly, at the first Board meeting following his installation in office.

He was content. There was no basic disagreement between them, and he had no objection to submitting to their authority if they, on their part, would grant him a free hand in actual management of the Institute. Until the sudden and inexplicable increase of blind infants in the forties, it was a comfortable and harmonious arrangement.

Even then there was no trouble at first. It was deplorable that there should be all these new blind children, but there was nothing the Board could do about that. What they *could* do

48

was to help supply them with writers when they reached school age, and there was no denying the usefulness of a larger market. The old near monopoly was gone now, with the American Printing House having revived the Hall Braillewriter and the Howe Press producing the new Perkins Braillewriter, a machine quite as efficient as the Taliferro and, like the Hall, considerably more durable. A little extra business would hurt nobody.

The difficulty was that, like most good things, the increase refused to stay within reasonable bounds. As the years passed and the retrolentals continued to be born, it became evident that before long the demand would exceed the Institute's capabilities unless some radical increase in production were achieved. Faced with the first real problem that had confronted him since his arrival at the Henhouse, Arthur turned to with enthusiasm, analyzed the situation, arrived at a solution, and ran head-on into a blank wall.

The trouble began with Ulysses. They were already manufacturing as many writers as he could adjust and repair, and that was as many as he had any intention of producing. He listened politely while Arthur outlined a system which would relieve him of his duties on the production line and free him to devote himself entirely to servicing the additional machines that would be returned to them; he listened, smiled, and flatly rejected it. He could not guarantee any new machine which he had not personally inspected, nor could he train anyone else to repair them. Mr. Evans must surely realize —

Arthur did, having anticipated this impasse. Casually, he advanced to his next position.

"You ever look over that report I sent you a couple of weeks ago, Ulysses?" he asked, busying himself with his pipe.

"From the Ohio School, you mean? It ain't worth the paper it's written on, Mr. Evans. Them fellas ain't mechanics. They're *schoolteachers*. How're they gonna redesign a machine's been working right since they was in kneebritches? It don't make sense."

"But they break."

"Durn right, they do, when they drop em. Ain't nothing I can do about that, Mr. Evans. And they ain't got sense enough to take care of them, all I can do is fix em up. Why, I'm still

49

usin the first one I ever made. Ain't never done nothin to it but clean it, neither,"

"But you're not blind, Ulysses."

"What's that got to do with it? The writer ain't neither. A machine's a machine, Mr. Evans. You drop it and it'll bust."

"The ones they modified at Ohio didn't."

"So they say. How do I know they didn't? A bunch of schoolteachers."

Ulysses, no longer young and gangling, glared at Arthur. He had ripened into a heavy-set, white-haired man in his mid-fifties, gentle, precise, and amiable. After his machinery, his greatest joy was in his fatherly, bachelor flirtations with the mature girls who womaned his assembly line. Now, however, the accustomed smile was missing from his lined, florid face, and he sat in Arthur's office, which was refurbished in business modern but as ascetic as in the Judge's day, plotted sedition, and feigned reason.

"Look, Mr. Evans," he said, "I reckon you don't understand. This is a production line. Them fellas, they just messed around with a couple of machines. Let's say they got one to where the head don't bust loose. I don't believe it, but let's say they did. But that don't mean nothin, don't you see? We gotta keep movin, turn out our quota every day, especially now you say they're gonna need all we can make. I can't fiddle with every machine like that, or we'd never get anything done. We got a good system now, Mr. Evans, it took me five years to get it goin but we've been doin it for damn near thirty years now, and I know it bettern the palm of my hand. And all that time they been usin my machines and likin them. You want I should mess it up now just because a couple of schoolteachers think they can do it better?"

"But your system can't produce enough writers, Ulysses. In a few years there will be blind children who need machines we won't be able to make. Machines we can't turn out because they're stacked up waiting for you to make final adjustments you can't get to because you're too busy repairing embossing heads that broke loose because that part of your machine isn't strong enough. That's the because, Ulysses, and that's why I want you to try the Ohio modification."

"And what happens to production while I'm fiddlin around with it?"

50

"But there's time, man. It's three years before the pressure will really be on us. By then you can have it worked out. It's only one part. Surely you can do that."

So they agreed, dishonestly, that Ulysses would work on it, both of them knowing they were only delaying a showdown each was confident of winning. Arthur counted on time and the Board's support, Ulysses on time and the Board's inclination. Unfortunately, Ulysses was proving right.

Not that the issue had yet been resolved. Under Arthur's relentless pressure, Ulysses had manufactured the new part, tested it, and found that it worked. And, as a concomitant, had created a constellation of technical difficulties so impressive that the Board, in whom Arthur's tentative probings had revealed a passionate commitment to business as usual, would certainly reject it unless he could manufacture an answer more speciously practical than any he or Zelda had yet been able to invent.

Last Friday's conference, the culmination of two years of fencing, had brought them to the verge of open warfare. Ulysses had been as rebellious as his practiced deference would allow. Without actually saying it, he had challenged Arthur to submit the issue to the Board for decision, a step which Arthur, without admitting it, had acknowledged his unwillingness to take.

So the matter lay as Arthur headed slowly back toward the Henhouse, following the traffic along the familiar route with an almost drunken clarity. At least, he thought as he slowed for the crossing where Harry Taliaferro had died, he had one advantage in today's session with Ulysses. For the first time in months he was his own man. Reaching a decision had given him back, however briefly, his old objectivity, and freed him, this day at least, to see the situation for what it was.

It all went together. Out of these months of turmoil at the Henhouse he had gained a new respect for the work to which they were all accidentally committed, a dedication which would no longer allow him to deny the importance of the service he ws battling to perform. But the real issue lay deeper. However the decision went, and he knew he could no longer postpone it, it was only part of an answer he alone could give, one which involved Vicki, Zelda, his children, and the whole world which, without really intending to, he had somehow built for himself.

51

That answer must now be faced. But beyond it lay a question far more fundamental, one which Zelda must now strengthen him to accept as she had freed him to pose it. It was simple enough.

Could Arthur Evans live with the consequences?

8

"Why, Arthur," Zelda said as she came briskly into his office, "a pipe. How nice."

"You noticed?"

"Noticed? My God, it's blue in here. I could smell it all the way back in the mail room."

"You like it?"

"Seems like old times. What happened?"

"I got myself back. Sit down."

He sat encircled by his appurtenances, like a man who has castled himself with possessions. How silly of me to think that, she thought. I hope I have sense enough not to tell him.

"You look like you just castled yourself," she heard herself saying. "Did you move your King first, or the tobacco jar?"

"Myself," he said with the relaxed grin she had almost forgotten. "Look, how quick can you set up a Board meeting?"

"An hour, I guess, allowing time to catch up with Doc Flint. But are you sure you want one? I got the idea Friday you were stalling for all you were worth."

"That was Friday. I've thought it over since. We've got to face it, Zel. If we lose, then at least we know where we stand. I've got to be able to level with people in New Orleans."

"And with yourself in Phoenix?" she said involuntarily.

"And with myself in Phoenix," he agreed soberly. "Especially with myself. Now get the boys lined up for me, will you? We won't call Ulysses in until you have it set. Tomorrow at ten. Here. Tell them it's urgent. Okay?"

"Roger," she said, unwinding in a fluid motion that thrust her breasts tight against her tailored white blouse. "Don't call me. I'll call you."

"One other thing," he said as she turned toward the door. "You have our reservations in New Orleans?"

"At the Monteleone, beginning Monday. And tickets on the sleeper Sunday night."

"Change it to Saturday. We'll go down Friday evening. We have some personal business we'd better tend to first."

The gaiety went out of her face, leaving a nakedness that excited, terrified, and shamed him. Her lean body, half-turned to receive another meaningless order, collapsed into a softness so yielding he thought she would fall, and her soul looked at him defenseless through her blind eyes.

"Zelda," he began.

"Did you mean that?" she said harshly, ignoring him.

"I meant it."

"Then why now? Now just like that, after all these years?"

"That'll take a while. We can talk about it in New Orleans."

"All right," she said tonelessly, turning back to the door. "I'll change the tickets."

When she had closed the door, gentling it shut with the same automatic touch that made her the Club's best woman volleyer, he leaned back in his armchair and let his eyes drift to infinity. His polished desktop stared back at him, the blotter pad a blur in its center, the gold-framed picture of Vicki and the children half repeating itself alongside his clock, his pipes and tobacco jar vague on the periphery. He felt empty, drained of the enthusiasm and purpose which a moment before had filled him with confident certainty. He was committed. Not that it had gone the way he expected. She might at least have looked a little happy about it.

The moment of her submission returned to him, the naked love he would never forget, and his annoyance dissolved in wonder and fear. Not even Vicki, that first time in the car, had ever looked at him like that. It had been like a mask peeling off, the bright smile stripped away to bare the eternal sadness beneath. Only the bone structure, deathly solid, prevented her whole face from turning inward. Flowing back to its beginning, down the caverns of her eyes. Jesus. Was he ready for that?

His loins stirred, and exultation again overwhelmed him. Impatiently, he thrust his chair back and began striding around the long room. It had been enlarged since the Judge's time. Toward the end of Harry's tenure they had knocked down the wall that had shut off Bessie's classroom and filled that half of the extended office with a table and chairs for Board meetings. The widow's symbolic gift on Arthur's accession had been complete new furnishings, the *piece de resistance* a large walnut table which replaced the cheap oak slab at which Harry, in a mixture of defiance and inherited penuriousness, had seated his new bosses. Arthur rounded it briskly and paused beneath a portrait of the Founder, painted in oil from a photograph taken the week before Bessie's accident. It had not been one of the Judge's best days.

"Well, you hungover old bastard," he said, grinning up at the only begetter of his technological woes, "stick around and you might see quite a show here yet."

He went to his desk to busy himself with paperwork, but his mind balked. As his hand shuffled letters from one pile to another, his thoughts raced toward vistas about which he knew only that they were limitlessly exciting. The exultation that filled him now was different from anything he had ever experienced. It was a growing sense of power, a certainty about something he did not even try to understand. How can one be certain about the unknown, precise about that which he cannot even begin to describe? But he was. He asked himself these questions, and his soul laughed. Something new had invaded him, something warm and sure and serene which made doubt not only impossible, but irrelevant. It was not merely that he believed. For the first time in his life, it seemed to him, he *was*.

Undeniably was. Christ, it was like rebirth. No wonder he didn't know what to do about it. Was that the way He felt when they rolled away that stone?

The image frightened him, and he dropped the pretense of work and sat staring off into the nothingness that had become everything. That thought was pure Zelda, with one important difference: it lacked her characteristic note of mockery. He had meant it. For that microsceond while the computer in his head made connections at whatever synapse registered megalomania, he had been the Being to whom, in his passionate childhood, he had once thought to dedicate himself, the unreal Reality about whom he had never since been able to think without embarrassment. Had been and, despite his fright, still was. The kingdom of the spirit was within him.

Jesus, buddy, he thought with no conscious contradiction, rising from his stillness to resume his lively pacing, Jesus, buddy, you're in too deep. An aura from the past descended on him, the odor of sanctity which had once pervaded the small Episcopalian church where he still attended but did not worship. The neat, vine-covered building, its velvet-lined pews dim in the stained light which filtered through its glowing windows, came briefly alive in him as it had been in the days when it was the symbol of the final mystery, mingled momentarily with his fear, and then died once again to become the meaningless site of his Sunday pilgrimages with Vicki and the children.

But that wasn't important. It was only an irrelevance, an automatic association which obscured the life within him. If, that is, anything could have obscured it. It burned inside him, calm and devouring. How long since he had thought of a phrase from the Testament as having any meaning for his own personal life? Not since the day over thirty years ago when Reverend Barnstable had told him that his personal habits did not suggest a young man destined for the ministry of God, the day he had taken his first real look inside that interior chapel where he had, with appropriately righteous satisfaction, nursed the flame of his dedicated calling, looked and found it empty and dark? Barnstable, that shrewd old fraud, had of course been right, and Arthur Evans had gone on to be a man like other men. Until Zelda.

The Kingdom of the Spirit is within you. It exactly described the light inside him now. Was it only the prospect of going to bed with a woman he had desired for years that kindled it? There had been affairs before, less premeditated, more casual —

The Thing inside him laughed again, and the grin it transferred to his lips brought him to a halt. Whatever his relationship with Zelda might become, *casual* was a word which would never describe it.

He had never been less certain of the future. His job, his wife, his children, the woman who would soon become his mistress—all the relationships which once had been anchored in the ordered security of humdrum existence were now unmoored, swept unpredictably out by waters on which he had never meant to venture. Why now, of all times, should he feel this overwhelming certainty in himself? When the others had been fixed, Arthur Evans had been nebulous. Now that everything else was in flux, he alone stood firm and unwavering at the center.

For the second time that morning he looked at his hand, observing its firm moulding, its new steadiness. *Invictus,* he thought. I am the captain of my soul. It just might even be. Suddenly he knew that he didn't want to understand, that it

56

was enough to have it, for however long, to accept as a gift from whatever gods there be the serenity which had transformed him. If in the end he were only Walter Mitty, well, Walter had his kicks too, and while the show lasted, he'd enjoy it. Afterwards could take care of itself.

He returned briskly to his desk and was working efficiently through his mail when the phone interrupted him. Zelda, her voice cheerfully impersonal. The Board meeting was set for ten tomorrow. Was he ready for his conference with Ulysses?

"Bring him on, baby," he said. "And bring your book, too. I may want a record of some of this."

He was studying the week's production report when they came in. Without glancing up, he waved them to their chairs and went on reading. When he had finished, taking time to check back against the year's cumulative totals on writers, he took off his reading glasses and looked at them. Ulysses, slouched like a bear in the straight modern chair, was staring intently at nothing. Zelda, her mask neatly repaired, glanced up instantly from her doodling and gave him her usual bright smile. Pride touched him, but he paid her the compliment of returning no more than a standard grin.

"Nice report," he said. "If you could do that every week, Ulysses, maybe we wouldn't have anything to argue about."

"Just worked out that way," Ulysses said defensively, accepting no compliments until he had tested them for booby traps. "I was all caught up on repairs this week so we got ahead on new ones. The girls work hard all the time."

"I know they do, Ulysses," Arthur said gently. "That's just what we've been talking about, isn't it? If you didn't have to spend so much time on repairs, we could turn out this many new writers every week."

Perceiving the trap he had been led into, Ulysses reddened.

"I told you already why the new head won't work, Mr. Evans," he said angrily. "Not in production, I mean. Time the girls finish messin around with it on the old machine, you'll get less writers than before."

"I'm sure that's true, Ulysses," he said. "Tell me, why do you think so?"

"I told you already. The whole thing's makeshift. It ain't what the machine was designed for. It's a jury rig, it'll take too much time to do, and it won't work right when we've done it. That's why."

"And so you're damned if you'll do it, right?"

"Didn't say that," Ulysses said, his little eyes bright with caution. "I just said it'll end up takin more time. And it would."

"It would indeed, Ulysses, because you've seen to that. Right?"

"I don't understand."

"You understand, all right, but we'll skip it. I'm just agreeing with you. Now I want to ask you something else."

"Ain't said nothing you got a right to accuse me about," Ulysses said as the idea began to penetrate. "Just said it'd take longer. Ask the girls and you don't believe me."

"I do believe you, Ulysses. For the moment. And I'm not accusing you of anything. Just stating a fact. Now let me ask you something else. Who owns the Taliaferro Braillewriter?"

"Why, the Board, I reckon. The Institute."

"Legally, yes. But who *really* owns it?"

"Well, I invented it."

"And turned your rights over to the Institute, to your credit. So who owns it now?"

"I reckon I don't understand you, Mr. Evans."

"Then I'll tell you. The blind children of America own that machine, Ulysses. We make it, but only as their trustees. It belongs to them, and to the dedicated people who'll transcribe books for them so that they can get an education despite the fact that they've lost the most human of all their senses. There are a lot more of these kids now, Ulysses, and there are going to be more yet, and I'm damned if I'll let you deprive them of their inheritance just because you're too bullheaded to change your ways. Do you understand that?"

He realized that he was shouting, and that for the first time in his years at the Henhouse Ulysses was looking at him with something of the fear he had once felt for the Judge.

"Now wait a minute, Mr. Evans," he said hoarsely. "There ain't nothin to get so excited about. I'm responsible for production, and I'm tryin to tell you what the problems are. I'm just doin my job, that's all. I want to help those blind kids just as much as you do."

"Then you just keep quiet a minute and listen, Ulysses,"

58

Arthur said, forcing his voice down and putting his hands in his lap to conceal their trembling. "You've been egging me on to take this to the Board because you think the Board will back you up. All right, I'm taking it to the Board. I've called a meeting for ten o'clock tomorrow morning. But before I do, there's one more thing I'm going to do, and I want you to make a record of this, Zelda, and of his answer. I hereby officially order you, Ulysses, as of today, to begin converting all new writers with the Ohio modification. Will you do it?"

"But it ain't that easy, Mr. Evans. It takes time to make a change-over like that."

"I know precisely how long it will take. You still have twenty-three of our trial order of that part on hand, and Watkins can supply us with another five hundred in two weeks. All you have to do is to get on the phone when you leave this office and give them the go-ahead. With the machines you already have in sub-assembly, I doubt we'll lose a day. Am I correct?"

"Well, sure, if everything goes right. But —"

"It's your job to see that everything goes right. You heard my instructions. Will you carry them out?"

"Well, sure, if you order me to, Mr. Evans. You're the boss."

"I'm glad you realize that, Ulysses. Now let me tell you one more thing. Tomorrow I'll give the Board a full report on my decision and the reasons for it. I will also give them a fair account of your objections and of my understanding of them. Maybe you're right that they'll back you up, but I doubt it, because if they do, they'll need a new President and General Manager. What I want to tell you is this. It's going to be up to me to see that these machines get out with the new modification, and I intend to see that they do just that. I'm going to be on your neck eight hours every day, and I want those machines to move just as fast as they did last week. Faster. If you think you and your girls can stall me, you've got another thought coming. I don't care if I have to fire every one of them. I don't care if I have to fire *you*. Those machines are coming off that line if we have to start all over from scratch. Is that clear?"

"Yessir."

"Very well. Now why don't you go along and get started? I'll check with you this afternoon."

Ulysses rose, suddenly a very tired old bear, and shambled toward the door.

"Just one more thing, Ulysses," Arthur said.

"Yessir?"

"There's nothing personal about this, and I want you to understand that. You're a good man, and I hope you'll be here a long time. But if you force me to choose between you and those blind kids, I'll take them every time. And don't you forget it."

When he had gone, Arthur leaned back in his chair and looked across at Zelda.

"Darling," she said, "you were wonderful. But are you sure you know what you're doing?"

"I thought your line was to be impersonal."

"You go to hell," she said. "Will the Board back us up?"

"The *us* I like. They'll back us for now. At this point, they haven't any alternative. But if I don't get those machines out, they'll find one."

"Then it's war between us and Ulysses?"

"All out war. Are you game?"

She looked at him levelly.

"I'm game for anything with you, Arthur Evans," she said. "You've never doubted that."

"No," he said, picking up his paper knife and testing the point against the back of his hand, "no, I guess I haven't. You've caught me looking Bramwell Wilson's tree, haven't you?"

"Several times."

"I don't feel that way now, you know."

"I can see. What do you feel like?"

"Like having my woman kiss me."

They met at the side of the desk, their thighs hard against the walnut plane that immobilized Vicki's picture and Arthur's pipes, lost in an embrace whose communion was more overpowering than anything either of them had ever known in bed.

9

Vicki was resting when Arthur came home. The screen door was locked, a signal that she was not to be disturbed, so he wandered around to the back of the house, returning a cheery wave from Lambert Brown, already puttering in his flowerbeds, with a reluctance he hoped did not show. The mess around the garbage cans was only half cleaned up, he noted sourly as he passed the neat grey box, its cover swung back as usual to reveal garbage cans whose covers were off as usual, a device he had designed, after Lambert's example and Vicki's protest, to conceal a mess even he found distasteful.

Rounding the corner on the cement walk splotched with red dust scuffed up from his ragged lawn, he bent automatically to pick up a bread wrapper, thought better of it, and climbed the steps to the long screened porch which, for most of the year, housed all their living except the rituals they performed in bedroom, kitchen, and bath. The door latch was still broken, he realized for the hundredth time; as a part of the outside, his side, it did not qualify for Vicki's ruthless efficiency, and would dangle unrepaired until at last, on impulse, he would stop at Gossert's and bring home the replacement it would take him fifteen minutes to attach.

He stepped into the cool neatness of Vicki's world. On the ceiling the huge fan turned slowly, stirring the languid air which bathed his oldest daughter, stretched invitingly, if you were Freedy Maynard, on a redwood chaise longue. To Arthur, in whom the garbage still festered, she presented a picture of well-tanned uselessness, clad in the standard uniform of denim shorts, sneakers, and sweat shirt.

"Damn it, Margie," he said, "didn't I tell you to clean up the garbage this morning?"

"Did."

"Did what?"

"Cleaned it up."

"Like hell you did. The cans and the box are all open and there's junk on the ground."

"That was Hank and Susie's part," she said, looking up from her comic book. "Annie and I did ours."

"Your job was to see it got cleaned up," he said, resisting an impulse to jerk her off the couch, "not to depend on the kids to finish it up for you. Now get up from there and do it right."

"Oh, don't be retarded, Dad," she said, dropping the magazine and stretching languidly. "You act as if the world's gonna come to an end or something over a little bit of trash."

"Your world's going to come to an end at suppertime for the rest of the week if that's not cleaned up in fifteen minutes," he said, picking up the comic book with the automatic gesture Vicki's regimen had instilled in him. "What's a sixteen year old girl doing with this kind of trash?"

"It's Susie's," Margie said, dropping one foot reluctantly to the floor. "I just found it here."

"And read it because you've nothing better to do," he said bitterly, turning toward the kitchen. "Now clean up that trash."

"Dad?"

"Yes."

"Can Freddy and I have your car tonight?"

"What's the matter with his?"

"The clutch went out or something spastic like that. He had to leave it at Brown's."

"That's no surprise," he said, a vision rising in his mind of Freddy's passionately destructive union with the vehicle which symbolized his manhood. "Why doesn't he take his father's?"

"Oh, he's going to a meeting or something. Or he says he is. You know how they are. They don't *want* Freddy to drive their car."

Bitterness over the whole organized conspiracy of adult stupidity darkened her tinsel voice.

"I didn't know Henry Maynard was that smart," he said, grinning in spite of himself. "What makes you think I want him to drive mine?"

"Well, you and mother are going to Shepherds tonight, and we figured you could both go in her car and we could use yours."

"Why don't you ask your mother for hers?"

"Oh, *Dad,*" she said, with a lapse into their old unity that touched him down where it hurt.

"Well, you can't have mine," he said, his evening suddenly

decided. "I've got to go over to Carters first to talk business with Captain Tom."

"But what'll we do?"

"Walk, I reckon."

"*Walk?*"

The unaffected horror in her voice released him again into his new freedom, and the smile he gave her was from Zelda's universe.

"Yes, walk," he said. "I realize that in two more generations all Americans will be born without feet and driver education will begin in kindergarten, but meanwhile you and Freddy still retain the appendages you despise, and if you're going anywhere tonight you can damned well use them unless you can persuade some other member of the roar and squeal set to carry you. Now get after that trash."

The kitchen was humid and quiet, despite the whir of the exhaust fan, and fragrant with Katy's cooking.

"What's for dinner, Katy?" he asked, pausing to acclimate himself to the dimness.

Katy was a country negress, set in her ways. She'd been raised by kerosene lamps, and electric lights had somehow become connected in her mind with the Jezebel ways of the sinful new generation. For reasons he had never been able to explain to his wife, the evening began to go wrong when Vicki, coming down from her nap or returning from an afternoon of bridge or shopping, snapped on the light before resuming command.

"But it's silly, Arthur," she had said when he protested. "Working in the dark like a mole or something. The poor thing will go blind, or maybe reach for the wrong seasoning by mistake. I'd like to listen to you then."

"Katy never seasoned anything wrong in her life," he had answered. "You know she always tastes everything before she puts it in. But it's her own world down there, Vicki. She's the one who has to do the work. Why not let her do it her own way?"

"I won't have it, that's all," Vicki said, ending the conversation. "It's *my* kitchen, and I like light."

"Meat loaf, Mr. Arthur," Katy said now, her grin flashing at him in the dusk. "And mashed potatoes and turnip greens and cow peas and sliced tomatoes. And chess pie for dessert."

"Reckon we won't starve," he said, with a smile that acknowledged their ancient intimacy. The real trouble between her and Vicki, a fact that they were all united in denying, was that she had been the Evanses cook since the days of Arthur's adolescence and had come to Arthur and Vicki only five years before, after his father's death and his mother's retirement to Mrs. Gray's. Thus effectively reestablishing Arthur as unacknowledged chief in the section of the house which Vicki regarded as peculiarly her own.

"Ice in the bowl there," Katy said as he headed purposefully toward the liquor cabinet.

"Good girl. Use a short one?"

"Little one for my stomach wouldn't hurt none," Katy said as he filled an old fashioned glass with ice and whiskey and poured her a shot in the small glass she had thoughtfully placed beside it.

"Where's everybody?" he asked, raising his glass in their habitual toast.

"Miss Vicki, she resting. Susie and Hank, they at the school playground. Annie, she gone somewhere I reckon Miss Vicki know about. Now you on and let me finish dinner. And put that bottle away so's I don't get tempted none."

He freshened his drink and went thoughtfully upstairs, stopping at the bedroom before proceeding to his study down the hall. Vicki slept peacefully under one of their new striped sheets. Naked, he thought from the way it moulded her body, and unwilling desire stirred in him. Defensively, he stared at the curlers he detested, crimping her blond hair into whatever patterns she had decided were right for the Shepherds' party. She would arrive looking rested and perfectly casual, with no sign of the indecently meticulous preparations which preceded her every public appearance.

You could trace the downward course of their marriage, he thought, from the night the curlers first appeared in her hair.

"Hello," she said, opening her eyes. "What time is it?"

"Half an hour till supper. I was thinking about waking you."

"I see you took time to get a drink first."

Since her father had taken to drink in the usual Phoenix

fashion, Arthur's drinking had become an obsession with her. The cocktail hour, once a time of mutual pleasure, had become another salient in their unending warfare. She still enjoyed liquor herself, usually drank more than Arthur at parties, and more often than not came home tipsy and eager for rutting. But in her world it was only men who turned to alcohol for solace in the curious spiritual menopause that assailed them in the middle years. Arthur having approached this climacteric, she was determined to save him from the fate to which, without her help, his sex would condemn him. As usual, her method was unflagging attack.

"If you have to drink, you might at least have waited for me," she said. "Do you need it as badly as all that?"

"And you might have been up to meet me," he said angrily, responding to provocations he had long since determined to ignore. "And with those damned gadgets out of your hair."

"I suppose you gave one to Katy too, as I have expressly asked you not to."

"I did. She enjoys one, and you couldn't pay her to take more. What's wrong with that?"

"Because I don't like it, that's what. Isn't what your wife likes more important than the cook's taste? She's independent enough already, without your doing your best to make a sot out of her."

"If you're so damned dissatisfied with Katy," he said, averting his eyes as she threw back the sheet and sat on the edge of the bed, naked and indifferent, "why the hell don't you fire her instead of complaining about her all the time?"

"How many of those have you had?"

"This is the first. But it won't be the last. Answer my question about Katy."

"You're not back at the Henhouse, lover boy," she said, going to the mirror and beginning to loosen a curler. "You can't order me around. I'm not your employee."

"Thank God for that," he said. "I'll see you after you get some clothes on."

"What's the matter, baby," she said, swinging her body toward him in an expert grind as he turned toward the door, "do I bother you like this?"

"No," he said, looking at her with the hate unleashed in his

65

eyes, "you don't bother me. You disgust me, you silly bitch."

He was brooding in his study, his second drink in his hand, when she came quietly in, cool and beautiful, with reconciliation in her eyes.

"Let's not fight, Arthur," she said, sitting down beside him. "I'm sorry I woke up snappish. Let's be together at the Shepherds tonight. It's too damned much of a strain if we're fighting."

"I don't want to fight," he said, "but you'll have to go on to Shepherds by yourself. I've got to stop over to see Tom Carter first. I'll be along later."

"What for? They'll have liquor, if that's what you want."

"I thought you didn't want to fight."

"Who's fighting? All he does is drink, for God's sake. Why else would you go over there?"

"Look, Vicki," he said, reluctantly letting her back into the place where he had installed Zelda, "we've got a crisis at the plant now, and I've got an important Board meeting in the morning. I need to talk to Captain Tom about it tonight."

"Why him? How can he help you in that wheelchair?"

"If you'd think with your head instead of your cunt for five minutes, you'd realize that Tom Carter, sitting emasculated and half-drunk in that wheelchair, still knows more about this town than anybody else in it. Before his accident he was the most active member of the Board, and he understands more about what I'm up against right now than all the rest of them put together. That's why I want to talk to him."

"You don't have to be vulgar about it," she said automatically. "Don't you know profanity is a sign of a limited mind? Come on downstairs and fix us a drink. If that's the way you're bound to go, I might as well enjoy helping you get started."

"Where's Annie, by the way?" he asked as she rose and smoothed her linen dress over her hips.

"At the Newtons for dinner and the night."

"Why didn't you tell Katy? She's expecting her for dinner."

"So what? She always makes twice as much as we need anyway, and then takes it home by the bag full to that menagerie that lives with her."

"Look, Vicki," he said, touching her unwillingly to hold her back, "not fighting, but I was serious about Katy. Why don't

66

you make up your mind either to fire her or accept her the way she is?"

"Arthur," she said, looking down at him with almost friendly contempt, "must you be so stupid? Of course I'm not going to fire Katy. She's the best cook in Phoenix, for one thing, and if I were ever foolish enough to let her go, one of our friends would grab her and I'd never hear the end of it. Besides the way it would look after all these years. But she's not easy to live with, as you wouldn't understand since you're still her little boy, and I take the brunt of it because I'm the one has to boss her as much as she can be bossed. Now will you come on down and fix me that drink? I'm suddenly dying of thirst."

She turned and marched gracefully out, her ass switching in the way that had ravished him twenty years before. He sat quietly for a moment, smelling her party perfume, and then grinned, rose, and bowed solemnly toward the door.

"Zelda, baby, it's going to be good," he said, drained his glass, and headed soberly down to the liquor cabinet.

10

Despite the anesthesia of drinks, dinner was the usual shambles, with variations. Susie and Hank, who had to be fetched at the last minute by Margie, continued some playground argument except during the intervals when Arthur's threats briefly quieted them. Margie, still in a state of shock from the prospect of actually walking, ingested her food in the kind of teenage trance he had come to recognize as impenetrable. Aside from occasional admonitions to sit straight, which she obeyed by twisting her shoulders vaguely upward, he left her to her bemusement.

Vicki was harder to tune out. Alcohol, he had long since concluded, went straight to her voice box. And to her snatch. Throughout the meal she inundated him with a flood of small talk that would have drowned out even the accomplished gabblers at her bridge club. Ignoring the children, somehow incredibly forking up food without interruption, mastication and vocalization synchronized into one continuous motion which fascinated and repelled him, she locked him, leg and eye, tight against this verbal sexual flow. After a few tentative efforts at escape, he began to eat slowly and with as much pleasure as he could muster in the imminent danger of being yanked from his chair, offering periodic cheerless smiles and interested grunts as earnests of his undivided attention.

As Katy's food took hold, the flood slackened until, with the appearance of dessert and coffee, she unlocked her leg from his, leaned back, and eyed him with somber aggressiveness.

"So you're going to let me go to the Shepherds alone," she said. "Hank and Susie, will you *please* shut up?"

"Just for a while," he said, testing the ground. "I'll be along before the party's really rolling."

"I know who'll be rolling," she said. "If you have to get drunk, why don't you do it with me?"

"Like now?" he said involuntarily.

"Don't be stupid. I don't mind your getting a little gay before dinner. It's fun. It's when you keep going that it frightens me. Do men always have to start running from something when they get your age?"

"Maybe they do," he said thoughtfully. "Maybe that's how it has to be. However, I'm not running tonight. I have to see Tom on business. I'm sorry you don't like it, but that's the way it is."

"Oh, all right," she said bitterly, starting on her pie. "I can't make you be sensible. But come on as soon as you can, will you? The Shepherds will think there's something funny. Especially after you come rolling in."

"John Shepherd hasn't had a thought for twenty years," he said. "And Elaine never had one."

"They were your friends before they were mine, dear," she said equably. "Now quit arguing and finish your pie. Katy wants to get on with the dishes."

This small conjugal victory restored her to good humor, and she kissed him pleasantly when he left, admonishing him to finish his business and hurry along to the party. Accepting her transmigrations as a part of an old game, no longer even wondering what endured down underneath, he replied cheerfully that he would and escaped into the fragrant night.

It was lovely. The gibbous moon hung low over the water oaks which lined their quiet street, its half light ballooning them into mysteries. The air was warm and tangible, caressing if, like Arthur, your blood was akin. He felt it as an embrace, in which his body moved joyfully against a faint, voluptuous pressure, a womb of passionate reassurrance. God, I love summer, he thought. How can people bear to live up north? On summer nights even flowers were marvelous, spicing the heavy air without demanding that you see the rows in which people like Lambert and Vicki sought to confine them. If it weren't for Freddy Maynard, he'd walk.

Of course, if he took the car there'd be time to stop at Zelda's. The memory of their kiss flowered in him, and with it a sudden, frantic conviction that Vicki was only waiting for the sound of his car to call him back and somehow cut him off from Zelda forever. Panicked, he eased silently into the car, started the engine in one burst, and roared away like Freddy Maynard in an average start. Even so he could hear the door flung open behind him.

Now what the hell did I do that for, he thought as he turned into the safety of the Macon Road and slowed to catch his breath. His heart was pounding, and his hands trembled on the wheel. Jesus, he thought, am I still as wound up as that? Maybe Vicki's right and I am drunk. I'd better go on to Tom's.

Nevertheless he stopped across from Zelda's, checking her car in the driveway and the light burning in the study. Maybe she was writing him.

Write me, baby, he thought, write me. Tell me you love me all the time we're apart. I'm more shook up than I thought, lover, and that serenity doesn't last so good when I'm back in the lion's cage. I need you, honey, and that's the truth.

The stop calmed him, but as he drove on, secure in the familiar cubicle of his car, guarded by the talisman of his glowing dash, he realized that it was not the meeting he wanted to talk with Tom about. It was Zelda.

Margaret greeted him at the door with a smile that turned sour when he told her his errand.

"He's upstairs," she said, stepping aside to let him pass. "I wouldn't count on being able to talk to him. He's already into his evening bottle."

But Captain Tom greeted him squarely from the center of the plateau.

"Arthur, by God," he said, "I'm delighted. I've been wanting to talk to you and you couldn't have come at a better time. I'm drunk enough to be happy and sober enough to communicate. Get a glass from the table and pull up a chair. There's ice and whiskey on the rack here. What's on your mind, boy?"

"I don't know exactly, Tom," he said, filling his glass. "I just know I need help. You're a man who thinks a lot. Did you ever have delusions?"

"That's a hell of a question to ask a drunk like me," the Captain said. "I have them most of the time."

"I don't mean that kind. I mean sober ones, relatively. Daylight ones, only this happened tonight."

"Like what?"

"Well, all of a sudden while I was standing on the sidewalk I got the idea that Vicki was trying to stop me from going out. I knew it so strongly that I sneaked in the car and drove off as fast as I could. But the delusion was that as I drove away I

70

heard her open the door and come running after me. I *heard* her, Tom, even though I know damn well she not only wasn't coming after me, she wasn't even giving me a thought. You know Vicki. Once I'm out she couldn't care less. But I heard her, Tom. I heard her as clear as I hear you now. You think I'm nuts?"

"I think a little more of the medicine I use too much of would help," the Captain said, pushing the bottle toward him. "You're so taut you're liable to snap any minute. Have another one before you answer the next question. It was Zelda you thought Vicki was trying to stop you about, wasn't it?"

"It was Zelda."

"What's between you, if I may ask?"

"Tonight? A kiss. Next week everything, I think, and I don't mean just going to bed. I mean all of it, and for good. Forever."

"It's like that, is it? For both of you?"

"For both of us."

"Then I guess I'd better talk a bit," the Captain said, putting down his glass, "and I reckon I'd better not drink any more until I finish. You stop me if I pick it up. Right?"

"Right."

"All right, then. I don't expect you understand how I feel about Zelda, Arthur, so I guess I'd better explain that first."

"I know you're fond of her."

"Fond of her, Jesus, man —"

"No."

"No what?"

"The glass. You took a drink."

"Shit. Here, you take it. And the bottle too. Put them on the table till I'm through. As I was about to say, fond of her doesn't say a thing. That girl's always been like a daughter to me, but now she's more than that. She's part of me. She *is* my daughter, Arthur. That's the part I need a drink to get through."

"You want one?"

"No, I want to talk. I don't mean my daughter physically. In mean she's taken the place of Emily. And that's something I never thought I'd admit to anybody."

He reached instinctively for his glass and pawed empty air.

"No wonder I don't last long," he said sourly. "Can't even

71

get through two consecutive sentences. I suppose you've heard how close old Fred and I were. He was my real father, every way but the biological one, understood me, encouraged me, helped me grow up. When we had daughters about the same age, I thought it was the greatest thing ever happened to me, especially when they turned out so much alike. But that was the trouble, I've finally realized. They were too much alike, except for one fundamental thing Zelda had and Emily didn't. You know what?"

"No, what?"

"Moral integrity. A simple, old-fashioned thing like that. I don't mean not going to bed or not taking a drink, the things these damned fools around here think are morals. Along with damned fools everywhere, I reckon. I don't know much about Zelda's habits, or Emily's either for that matter, except they both had sense enough to have their kicks. They're alike in that. That's their business. What I mean is the moral courage to be honest with herself. Zelda's got it and Emily hasn't, and now I think I'll have that drink, because I'm almost through."

He drained his glass, refilled it, looked at it, and put it down again.

"Greatest companion in the world," he said. "Too damned bad I don't have the sense to use it right. You understand what I'm talking about, Arthur?"

"I understand it in Zelda. I never knew Emily that well, Tom, but Zelda's got it. I'll guarantee you that."

"Damn right she has, boy. And I'll tell you something else. Emily's lost now, maybe killing herself, because she didn't have it and married a man who did, a man too big for her and she doesn't know what to do about it. Not what I'd worry about with you and Zelda, though. Worry the other way. I'm not so damned certain she's not too big for *you*."

"Shove that bottle this way, will you, Tom?" Arthur said. "I ought to resent that remark, but I guess I don't. Fact is, I'm afraid you're right. Even though I'm a solid citizen in this town, a successful executive, worker for civic good, and pillar of the community. Ask anybody. Even my wife."

"Solid shit," the Captain said. "Go on, finish it up and get one from the cabinet there behind you. You're just as solid as I am, buddy, and that's not saying much. You're too smart to buy the crap they call respectable in this town and too chicken to get the hell out and be what you ought to be. That about right?"

"I'm afraid you got it."

"Damn right. Got something else too. Zelda, she's not like that. She came back because she wanted to, but nobody's got his hooks in her like Vicki has in you. You think I don't know how it is with you and Vicki? Hardly know her, you might think, I'd retired when she came to town, but I've got her taped, and you too. When she whistles, you dance, buddy, and that's the story. How come you think you're having traumas, at suppertime right in your own front yard? You think Zelda's a girl will put up with that if she decides to line up with you. You got some changing to do, Art, and it may hurt. Drink up."

"Now wait a minute," Arthur said, pouring another before passing the Captain the new bottle. "It's not as bad as that. I've led my own life. I do what Vicki wants to keep her quiet."

"Led your own life, have you? Then how come you want to run off with Zelda?"

"Who said I wanted to run off with her?"

"I did. But you do, don't you?"

"Yes," Arthur said slowly, feeling a sudden peace. "God help me, but I do. Never admitted it before, Tom, but Jesus how I do. Pass that bottle."

"Get drunk if you don't watch it," the Captain said. "Not too long now, way we're going, and I'll slide off the plateau."

"You'll what?"

"Manner of spaking. Get drunk, I mean. You know I do every night. I'm gonna slow down, boy. Not often I get a chance to talk like this."

"Damn if *I* will. Vicki said I'd get drunk tonight. Okay, so she's right. Couldn't happen to a nicer girl."

"Be my guest. But the hell with Vicki. Zelda's who we're talking about."

"Then let's talk about Zelda," Arthur said, downing half his drink before leaning forward into his best hortatory stance. "So she has more guts than I do. Maybe I just haven't used mine yet. I'm learning, Tom. I tell you, that girl does things to you. Jesus, I've found out what I really believe about most of the things that matter to me since she began educating me. Look

73

at today. This morning I rode by Bramwell Wilson's oak tree and damn if I didn't want to stop and do myself in too. I about got my ass knocked off in traffic and rode a mile past the Henhouse without even realizing it. So I pulled off and said, what the hell's the matter with you, Evans? You know what it is, I told myself. It's Zelda. You know goddamn well you want her. Why don't you admit it? So I went straight back to the office and told her."

"That's good," the Captain said gravely.

"Damn right it's good. It's wonderful. I felt so good I took on Ulysses and did what I should have done months ago. Told him he'd better get on with changing over the writer or I'd can him. Meant it, too."

"Futral still gumming up the works?"

"Same old shit. Matter of fact, that's why I came to see you. I ordered him to begin a modification that'll speed up production and mess up his little system, and I've called a Board Meeting tomorrow to give them the word."

"What's all the rush? Machines for retrolentals?"

"How do you know about that?"

"I read up here when I'm not stiff. Been messing around in the field too long not to keep up with it. You want to know whether the Board will back you up?"

"Thought I did. But I know that answer, for now anyway. Really wanted to talk about Zelda."

"Damn right you did. But lemme say something before we get back to her. They'll back you now, all right. They have to. But watch Ulysses, boy. He's shrewd, and he won't stop at anything. He'll have you out on your ass in three months if you don't beat his brains out first. Not that it might not be the best thing at that."

"How do you mean?"

"What are you doing after this?"

"Meet Vicki at Shepherds. Big fat dull party."

"You'll be stiff."

"That's what she said."

"Then why not stay here? We can keep on talking and you won't have to worry about her till tomorrow."

"Christ, she'll blow a gasket."

74

"Let her. She'll have more than this to blow about before it's over. What do you say?"

"I'd like to. But Jesus, I hate to talk to her."

"We'll let S. T. do it. Listen."

He lifted a phone from its cradle on the chair arm and pressed a button in a panel beside it.

"All the comforts of home," he said. "S. T.? Look, Mr. Evans is staying the night. Lay out some pajamas and stuff in the guest room. And look. Call up Mrs. Evans at the Shepherds and tell her he's tied up in a business conference that may take half the night and that he'll be staying here afterwards. Tell her he'll call her from the office in the morning. Yes, young John. Christ, I know she'll scream, but make her happy. I don't care how you do it, just do it. No, call her right now. She'll have had enough to be mellow and it's not so late that she'll be furious. That's the idea. I knew you'd figure it out. And look. You'd better bring up some more ice. This conference is pretty demanding."

"What the hell's he going to tell her?" Arthur said when the Captain hung up. "There's nothing'll pacify Vicki if I don't show up when she's told me to."

"One gets you ten S. T. will," the Captain said. "He can charm a rattlesnake."

"Precisely the situation," Arthur said. "Only this one always bites."

"Not S. T. she won't. After he explains how Doc Flint came over, and how we're all three in a high level conference and can't be disturbed, after he gives her the business in that sincere voice of his she'll go home after the party and sleep like a baby."

"You think she'll fall for that phony line? You don't know her. She'll have Doc Flint on the phone just to check up, and then where'll we be?"

"You don't know *her*, my boy," the Captain said, reaching for his glass, "and your technique is sadly in need of improvement. In the first place, she won't call him. Not this time. She's still too proud. Even if she did, she wouldn't get him. Not even his wife knows where Doc is, and he might as well be here. Tomorrow I'll have him squared away so that he'll swear on a stack of condoms he was here half the night. Now take that glass

75

and let's toast the future. All this intellectual exercise has got me so damn sober I'm good for the night."

"Tom."

"Yes, Arthur."

"What did you mean by saying that it might be for the best if Ulysses put the skids under me?"

"Just this, son, and I'm glad you asked me while I'm so abnormally clear-headed. Phoenix, your Phoenix that is, hates Zelda. You know that, don't you?"

"Hates her? Why in hell should they do that?"

"Jesus, Art, don't you know anything? Zelda could tell you. They hate her because her father was poor white and she's turned out to be more of an aristocrat than any of them. Mrs. Taliaferro and all the other little pissant snobs you and Vicki pal around with can't stand that. They can't forgive her looks, or her voice, or her brains, or her education, and most of all, boy, most of all they'll never forgive her if she takes you. They will scream so loud you can hear them from here to Macon, and they'll keep after you both until one way or another they've killed you off. If you want Zelda, you've got to give up Phoenix and everything you have here. If you're not ready for that, for God's sake, for your sake as well as hers, don't get involved with her. And to pay you a compliment, I'm beginning to think it may be that way for you too."

"Thanks for that much."

"We'll see. So if it takes losing your job to wise up, maybe it's for the best. That's what I meant. Now the hell with being serious. I haven't had a night like this for years, and I mean to enjoy it. Tell me about that damn brailler while I'm still sober enough to understand it. Maybe I'll have an idea or two about it at that."

They settled down to shop talk and serious drinking. Three hours later, when their campaign had progressed into incoherence and parody, the Captain pressed the button which summoned S. T. to bed them down, and they raised their glasses, laughed, and, like lovers, slid together off the plateau into nothingness.

11

"Darling," Zelda said, "when did you first know?"

Lovers now, they sat at the bar in the Old Absinthe House, locked in the ancient unity which is the world's illusion and the chosen's truth.

"Know what?" Arthur said. "How good you'd be in bed?"

"Was it really good, darling?" she said, leaning over to bite his ear.

"Which time?"

"The first time, stupid, before you knew what I was like."

Was it good? How answer that immemorial question, the maid's plaint when, bedeviled by the malicious tales of envious old wives, she turns fearfully to her lover and whispers, was I good, darling, was I really good? Lover of tradition though he was, Zelda had taught him in a single act of passion the criminal stupidity of a superstition nurtured by those incapable of love — the myth that the first time is best, and that after that it all runs downhill.

Had it been better? Technically, no. Vicki was a master mistress, and they had had years to adapt to each other's every nuance. But in intensity, and most especially in communion, it had been an experience of a new order, promising a future which filled him with wonder and fear.

"It was what life ought to be about, Zel," he said at last. "Does that answer your question?"

"I'll rape you right here if you keep on talking like that," she said, "but no, it doesn't answer it. I want to know when you first knew we were coming to New Orleans for this."

"About fifteen minutes before I told you."

"And even then you had to start me arranging that meeting first? You bastard."

"Well, it was important, wasn't it? To both of us. And you got to admit it was a success."

It had been that. It had gone just the way he and Captain Tom had plotted it, another interlude in a day inexorably serene.

He had wakened with absolutely no hangover and gorged himself on the sausage, eggs, and biscuits which Essie, Katy's friend and only rival, lavished on him. When he called Vicki at nine-thirty, she sounded more like a helpmate than a wife. The Captain and Doc Flint had both talked to her, and she was timid with solicitude, almost abject in her apologies for underestimating the crisis he must now face alone. Zelda had stopped in briefly for the touch that joined them, hand-holding desperately over the desk as she dropped the mail, their grasp sliding up their forearms to lock them like wrestlers in an act of love.

Only yesterday, he thought. An eternity.

Doc Flint had taken the ball. He arrived ten unbelievable minutes early, settled his already rumpled seersucker suit in Zelda's chair, and grinned at him.

"Didn't expect me now, did you, boy?" he said over the eternal cigarette that drooped from his lip.

"That's for sure, Doc," Arthur said. "I'd have made book against it."

"Odds were with you," Doc said. "Bet it every time. But Tom called me this morning, and I figured I'd better come along."

"Thought he did after I talked to Vicki. I appreciate that."

"Think nothing of it. Goddamned women'll take over the country if we don't get organized. She act all right?"

"Perfect. Completely out of character. First time I ever stayed out all night, and she's apologizing. I don't see how you did it."

"It's the doctor image. Never fails. Even when you screw them they figure it's therapeutic. Though I will say S. T. and Tom had her softened up. You got the right friends, boy."

"I'm beginning to realize. I guess I should have sooner."

"Takes a while. What's with Ulysses now? Tom tells me you have to change his system to get out writers for all those kids that went blind in oxygen therapy, and Ulysses wants to block it."

"That's about it. I'll explain in detail at the meeting, but the point is unless we modify the machine so it'll break less, he'll never have time from repairs to check enough new ones. But that means changing his design, and he'll fight it all the way."

"Does he have to check all the new ones?"

"You'll never stop him from that, Doc. I don't even know that we should. It's his machine, and he knows it better than anybody in the world. He can tell a loose nut just from looking at it."

"Then he'll have to accept the change. You present it and I'll back you. But remember this, Arthur. It's up to you to make it work. Everybody on this Board but me think's he's a businessman, and they want this nonprofit institution to operate in the black. Don't matter whether it makes sense, it's their chance to look like smart operators. If production goes down, there won't be anything I can do to help you. You've got to whip Ulysses into line. Can you do it?"

"I don't know. All I know is I've got to try."

"So be it," Doc said as the buzzer rang. "It's ten on the dot, and that'll be Henry Maynard. You could make book on him too, but I don't think you'd enjoy the work."

It had gone just like that. After Arthur's initial presentation, Doc had taken over, speaking with surprising eloquence about the tragedy of the retrolentals and the responsibility of the medical profession and of the Taliaferro Institute for the Blind to make amends, however inadequate, to the victims of a therapy in which eagerness to save lives had overrun scientific caution. The Board listened with the customary apathy of those who govern but do not understand. Any change was deplorable, but if it meant so much to Doc and Arthur, there was no harm in trying it as long as it didn't get out of hand.

Only Henry Maynard, pedantically jealous of his authority as chairman, raised the objections that spoke to their secret hearts.

No one, he began, would deny the Institute's responsibilities in a field in which it had performed such long and noteworthy service. Its whole history testified to its dedication. But was it sound business, was it really in the interests of those unfortunates whom they had come into being to serve, to make changes in a system which had proven itself over the years, without first making certain that there was not another way, perhaps through other suppliers, of procuring the additional machines which would unquestionably be needed? And what about the possibility, unlikely but nevertheless an alternative

79

which sound practice required them to consider, that the pro-
posed changes might actually lead to a decrease in production?
What then?

Doc got them past that one. Arthur sat smiling and non-
committal in his place at the far end of the table, occasionally
looking up past Henry Maynard's tight-lipped face to the Judge's
portrait, slack-jawed but incorruptible on the wall which contained their compromises, while that rumpled old sinner, briefly
reborn into the idealism which had first seduced him into medicine, shamed his compatriots into a momentary admission of
their responsibilities and secured unanimous approval of the
Ohio modification.

There were, of course, qualifications. The entire question
was scheduled for review at a special meeting three months
hence. In the event of any unexpected difficulties, it would be
Arthur's responsibility to call a Board meeting immediately.
And at forthcoming meetings of the American Association of
Workers for the Blind in New Orleans, he was instructed to
confer with the production managers of the American Printing
House for the Blind and the Howe Press of the Perkins Institution, in order to explore ways of increasing the production of
writers through these sources. The meeting broke up in sweet-
ness and artificial light, a success, unquestionably, but a tenu-
ous one.

"Another round, sir?" the bartender said.

"By all means," he said, returning to meet Zelda's mocking
grin. "And what the hell are you smirking at?"

"You. I was waiting for you to come back. Where've you
been?"

"Back at the Henhouse. Where else?"

"Doesn't matter as long as it's not somebody else's bed. Been
reviewing the unqualified success of that meeting you were just
bragging about?"

"As usual, lover, you're right on the nose."

"Then try this one on for size. Didn't it strike you that Henry
Maynard was unusually well informed at that meeting?"

"It's hard for me to think of Henry as well informed about
anything, but it's true, now that you mention it, that he was
sharper than he should have been."

"Damn right he was. Now think about this one. Where do

you think Ulysses was visiting that evening you were communing with Captain Tom and the whiskey bottle?"

"With Henry, you mean? Don't be silly. A snob like Henry wouldn't let Ulysses in the house."

"Darling," she said, lifting her martini in toast before taking a long sip, "it's too bad you're not a peon too. Damn, these are good. If you were, you might understand this town and phonies like Henry Maynard a little better, and know more about what we're up against at the Henhouse. Shall I clue you?"

"Clue ahead."

"Okay. Of course Henry won't let Ulysses in the house, socially, but he'll welcome him any time he can *use* him, especially against you and me. You committed the unpardonable sin at that meeting, lover, and Henry could smell it coming the minute Ulysses called him up and said he had something to talk over with him. You got out of hand, my boy, politely and with Doc running interference, but out of hand just the same, and Henry won't forgive you for that. As Chairman of the board he's Boss, and he intends to keep it that way. He has to be Boss even though he doesn't know a goddam thing about the operation because it's one more way of proving to himself that Henry Maynard is important. When you questioned his authority, you became dispensible. Add that to the fact that he hates us both, and we've got quite a situation on our hands."

"Now wait a minute," Arthur said, finishing his drink and signaling for another. "What the hell are you talking about? Tom told me they hated you, and I didn't believe that. But why should Henry hate me? Our families have been friends for years, and we've always gotten along. I've never liked the bastard, I'll admit, but he's enough older than I am that we've never been around in ways he'd find it out."

"He knows, all right. People like Henry expect you to dislike them. But that's not the reason he hates you. You listen to your poor white woman now, sweetie, and get this through your thick, beautiful head once and for all. After, that is, I finish this drink."

She drained her glass and handed it to the bartender, approaching with fresh ones, with a smile that clutched Arthur's heart.

"These are marvelous," she said. "What makes them so good?"

"Gordon's gin," the bartender said, abandoning his tourist manner in the face of her vividness. "Noilly Prat vermouth, lemon twist, and a touch of absinthe on the rim of the glass. And the fact that you're so happy with the gentleman here."

"Does it show that much?"

"Like a searchlight," the bartender sid, uniting them with a smile. "This one's on me, folks. And good luck to you."

"Why, thanks," Arthur said.

A sudden wild joy filled him, an overwhelming happiness that this bartender should recognize their love and be humanized by it, and he grinned back with none of the embarrassment he usually felt in displaying his feelings before strangers.

"How about having one with us?" he said. "Just for luck. It's an occasion, and we'd like to toast it with you."

"I reckon it's that time of day," the bartender said, reaching back without looking to settle his hand unerringly around the neck of a bottle of Old Fitzgerald, from which he poured a sizable slug into a plain glass. "Cheers," he said, "and may all your troubles be little ones."

Zelda giggled.

"Now there's a complication we hadn't figured on, darling," she said. "No, I'm afraid all our troubles are pretty big right now, uh —"

"Louis," the bartender said. "You folks just passing through?"

"We're here for a meeting of workers for the blind," Arthur said. "You'll have plenty of them in here from tomorrow on. Blind drunk too, I suspect."

"The blind, eh," the bartender said, according the joke a routine smile. "Whatta you know. My sister's got a kid born blind. Something they did wrong when it was in an incubator, or what the hell ever you call it. Happened in the best hospital in the city too. How do you figure a thing like that?"

"Retrolental fibroplasia," Arthur said. "Wasn't anything the hospital did wrong. The excess oxygen caused it, only they didn't know it then. How old's the child?"

"Eight. Bright as hell, too. And pretty as a picture. Don't look blind at all. She's up at the Louisiana School for the Blind, but when she's home for vacation, I take a day off just to spend it with her. You ought to see what that kid can do. I bought her one of these braille typewriters for Christmas, ordered it from a place up in Georgia —"

"Hey, that's us," Zelda said, bouncing up and down on the stool. "The Taliaferro Institute for the Blind. We make them. Arthur here is President. What do you know?"

"Arthur Evans," Arthur said, extending his hand. "She had any trouble with the machine?"

"Glad to meet you, Mr. Evans," the bartender said. "That's great work you're doing. Not a bit of trouble that I know. But it would've done your heart good to see how happy she was with it. You'd think I'd given her the U. S. mint."

"She will the first time it gets knocked off the table or somebody bumps it right. That's what Zelda and I, Miss Huckaby here, were just talking about. We're changing the design of the machine to prevent that. I want you to keep my card, Louis, and if anything goes wrong you write me personally. I'll see she gets a new machine by return mail, one that won't break. Got it?"

"That's mighty decent of you, Mr. Evans," the bartender said, taking out his wallet and tucking the card carefully inside it. "I got a lot cards here besides all the ones they stick on the walls and ceiling, but this is the first one I ever kept. Janie'll get a big kick out of my having met you."

"No more than we," Arthur said. "Girls like Janie are what we're in this for. I guess we'll vote again, Louis."

"Oh, darling," Zelda said when Louis had moved down to busy himself with mixing, "I love you for that. I like it that when you got smart enough to make love to me you also had found out what the Henhouse really ought to be for. You really never knew before, did you?"

"I'm afraid I never really knew anything until you," he said. "What was it you were going to tell me about Henry Maynard?"

"Oh," she said, taking both his hands in hers and caressing him with her beautiful eyes. "I'd forgotten. Here's what you don't understand, darling. This town's built on a caste system that's phony as a three dollar bill."

"This town? You mean New Orleans?"

"I mean Phoenix, stupid. Thanks, Louis. Now you shut up and listen. I can say this because I began at the bottom, and

83

it cost me a lot of pain to learn how to look at it objectively. Or fairly objectively. The point is that by what people like the Maynards call their own standards, there are only four families in town that qualify as good. The Carters, the Wilsons, the Evanses and the Ingrahams. In that order. The rest of them are all poor white, just a generation or two back. A few years ahead of the Huckabys on the same route. They hate me because Fred and I made the jump too quick, especially me, because he never pretended to anything but what he was. I beat them at their own game, if you'll forgive my saying so, and it kills them. As for you, Henry Maynard hates you because you've the real thing and he's a phony. He knows it, and it never occurs to him that you're too simple minded to know it too. As long as he's your boss and you're an obedient vassal, that makes it even better. It's another triumph for old Henry, another way of making himself believe what he knows isn't true. But once you start being troublesome, then he's got to get rid of you, because you just might assert yourself and put him in his place, and he'd rather kill you than let that happen. Now do you understand?"

"It doesn't keep him from letting his son court my daughter."

"Of course, it doesn't, Art. Can't you see? That's a step up for Freddy, even if Henry gets you fired from the Henhouse it's still a step up, and he'll be for it all the way. He'd even accept a shotgun marriage if it was to an Evans. But you and me at the Henhouse, and it is me too because I'm your assistant even though he doesn't know anything yet about what else is between us, why that's a different matter, and he'll use Ulysses and the whole damned board, except Doc, to crush us. That's what you are up against, lover boy, that's what you put your foot in when you gave Ulysses the works that day in your office."

"So that's what Captain Tom meant when he said that if I wanted you I'd have to give up everything I have in Phoenix and clear the hell out."

"Did he say that, bless him? Well, he's right."

"Is that what you want to do, Zel?"

"I want to do what you want to do, Art. Truly I don't give a damn as long as we're together."

"It's not easy, baby."

"It's not easy to fall in love with a new world after you've

84

already built an old one. That's the Columbus syndrome. How about your children?"

"I wish I knew. I love them, you know, even though they're all managing to irritate me right now, especially Margie, she's the one that's going with Freddy Maynard and she used to be the closest to me. I just don't know. I feel a hell of a responsibility, but the more I grow into a new life with you, the more I seem to grow away from theirs. Vicki and I don't do them any good together any more, and I know that when we hit our first real crisis we'll begin doing them positive harm."

"What about Vicki?"

"We're strangers, Zel. Enemies, I almost said, but maybe that's too strong."

"Loving enemies."

"I wish we were even that. We haven't communicated in years."

"How about in bed?"

"That bothers you?"

"Damn right it bothers me. How would you feel if I were in bed every night with somebody else?"

"There've been nights."

"There have been. But it's a little different."

"Look, baby," Arthur said, signaling to Louis, "let's have one more and go. For the first time, I think in our whole relationship, I'm ahead of you. And by God it makes me feel good. Maybe eventually we'll get to where we ought to be, where I'm ahead of you most of the time."

"Don't exercise your new-found gift for words on me, lover," she said, leaning over to rub her cheek against his arm. "How about you and Vicki in bed?"

"All right," he said, "I'll tell you. It's sex. It's good sex too, I won't deny that, and from Vicki's point of view I guess that's enough. I know she enjoys it, and she's got no interest in anything more. But it's not enough for me, Zelda. I want something more. When Vicki and I make love we're both alone, each satisfying himself and the other. But I want it together, I want communication, communion every minute. I never really had it before, but I know it exists. I knew, and I can't explain to you how, that it would happen with you and me. And it did. And it's why I have to be with you."

"Then it really was good?"

"I told you already, baby, and by God I'm still ahead of you, it's what life ought to be about. We have things to learn, about our bodies, and each other, and all the things we can do and the ways we can do them, but the basic thing, the thing I'm certain most people just don't have, that was there from the beginning, and I hope to hell we never lose it."

For the first time in their lives, she looked at him almost with reverence.

"Darling," she said, "I knew there had to be a reason why I fell in love with you. Now I'm starting to find out. I begin to feel we have business back at the hotel. Have you settled with Louis?"

"Just one more thing," he said. "It'll only take a minute. You asked me what I wanted to do. I'll tell you what I really want. I admitted it the other night to Captain Tom. I want to run away with you and say the hell with everything. But I'm not going to do it, Zel, and the reason, funny as it may seem, is right back at the Henhouse. I've theoretically been Manager for twelve years, and you're right, it's only just now that I've understood what it's about. This battle is serious for me, and I've got to see it through. My mind tells me we'll lose, and we probably will. Ulysses is a tricky bastard, and the whole goddamn set up is rigged against us. And I'm now willing to believe your analysis of Henry is right. But all that doesn't matter. I can't quit until I've lost, until we've done everything the two of us together can do. If I quit now, and let kids like Janie down without really trying, I'll lose the manhood I'm just beginning to find, Zel, and what the hell will I have accomplished then for anybody? So I'm sticking. Are you game?"

She looked up at him with eyes heavy with tears.

"Damn you, Arthur," she said, "I love you enough already without your having to break me up. You don't have to make it so good it frightens me. Just tell me something. When are you going to get together with the boys from Howe and the Printing House?"

"I thought we'd all have lunch tomorrow or Tuesday. Hell, I already know the answers. Howe is just getting going again after their first lot, and the Printing House can supply whatever they're called on for. The trouble is, people would rather

86

have a Perkins or a Taliaferro than a Hall, and it's our job to see that they have that choice."

"Then the rest of the day is ours?"

"All ours. Including the night."

"Then, my boy," she said, her eyes shining behind the film of tears, "I think perhaps first we'd better go back and make sure the maid fixed my bed up properly. Then I feel for Arnaud's, and a couple of bars I've explored under dubious circumstances I'll probably never admit to you, and then Fats Pichon at the other Absinthe House, and then the French Market and back to check on your bed, and after that, goddamn you, it's up to you. Do we go?"

"We go," he said, and picked her up from the stool, kissed her, waved to Louis, and went hand in hand out into the brilliant summer afternoon.

12

For Vicki that summer had stood still. How could it have been, she sometimes wondered afterwards when they both lived only in her memory, that it had seemed so peaceful when the explosion was so nearly at hand? One meaningless day like any other, a year or two afterwards, she bought a reproduction of John Steuart Curry's *The Line Storm* and hung it over the bed that once had been Arthur's. It was only much later that she realized why. It must have been like that, she told herself then, racing while they seemed to stand still toward the shelter they never reached, the storm exploding around them while its lightning shook her world.

When had she first begun to suspect? After that trip to New Orleans, it should have been, when he came back with that bitch's smell on him and a look in his eye that would have told her had she the sense to see. Downright jaunty, so that he glittered as he walked. But she hadn't known. She'd loved him even, knowing inside her in the stillness an almost stirring of the feeling that once had been real, the sense that her man breathed and walked, and could touch her with his commanding hand.

God damn you, Arthur, she thought, the old hate smouldering in its ashes, why, of all people, did you have to pick her? That cheap, on-the-make bitch. A poor white Radcliffe whore, using the thing between her legs in the immemorial fashion of the tow-headed tribe that had spawned her, to steal from her betters what was not hers by right.

It wouldn't have had to go that way if it hadn't been her, darling, she thought. I loved you, you know, and I could have put up with anything that didn't degrade me. You understand that, don't you? You must have known it was Margie I had to think about, as her father you'd have wanted me to put her first.

So she had, and the empty house was her legacy, Margie gone now and Annie and Susie and Hank already itching, it often seemed to her, for the departures which had become the universal fate of their clan. Except Old Vicki. Who endured.

It had not been that way then. She had existed, damn it, unknowing perhaps and certainly unsuspecting, while they wove the web with which they had vainly plotted to deceive her. The fools.

Those months after his return from New Orleans had been wonderful. There was new vigor in him, give the bitch credit for that, a certainty that made life better for them all. He made love to her with enthusiasm as well as efficiency, asking no impossible union but enjoying the physical fact with gusto and tenderness. Not since their first years had they had such a passionate interlude. Almost, until she understood what had really been happening, she began to think he had grown up at last, and even considered letting down the bars.

Thank God she hadn't been quite that stupid. Knowing in time, she had escaped that final degredation and kept the temple of her soul inviolate. But God, it had been close. Another month, and she might have had him trampling in, smiling false assurance and wearing that bitch on his balls.

Thinking was dry work, and she went into the kitchen to fix another of the drinks without which the days no longer seemed endurable. Watch it, Vicki, she told herself automatically. It's only ten o'clock. A hell of a lot of day left to go.

Not that she had a thing to worry about. No one suspected, not a bloody, stupid soul. God, wouldn't it shock them if they knew? Old Vicki, good, respectable, clean-cut, clean-living Vicki, brave little wronged heroine of our late, much enjoyed, highly deplorable scandal, nipping away in the kitchen from the time she got up until she fell into bed.

But they didn't know. And they wouldn't. Thanks to an iron constitution, vodka, and the kind of will power most of them couldn't imagine, through which she paced herself to walk confidently along the edge until she dove intentionally into sleep. At parties she was her old self, a trifle gaunt from the suffering that was her justification but brave and gay in spite of it, coming home soberer than in the old days because there was no one to lean on now and she was afraid to let herself go.

Afraid. Oh Arthur, she thought, feeling the liquor warm inside her but finding no comfort in it, did you have to do that to me? Whatever else was wrong with me, I was never afraid.

Stupid certainly, and not running maybe because I didn't know enough, but never afraid. Who now lives with memories she cannot bear to face, and hides in the bottle that works only because she makes it work but is no substitute for the reality that might have been.

Shit. You're getting too damn close, Vicki girl, she thought, and for why? Who gives a damn when you knew, or why you knew, or how? You knew, and you all did what you had to do, and that's that. Nobody's to blame, worse luck, it's just the way it was. All we have to do is live with it, those of us who can. And tough tit for those who can't.

But I can't really, darling, she thought with sudden desperation, I didn't mean to do it that way, you must know that. I didn't because I knew I couldn't afford to lose you, darling, I couldn't bear for you to leave me then. Or ever.

Ever. And what was that? A meaningless interlude between drinks. A pimple on the ass of nothingness. This long day could go to hell, she decided, and Phoenix and tonight's dinner at the Brown's along with it. It would all be here when she came back, and today, above all, she must forget.

She drank.

13

"Oh darling," Zelda moaned, "if you only knew what you do to me."

"I know," Arthur said as he drove them with savage tenderness toward their passionately delayed fulfillment, "goddamn right I know. And I love it."

"But it's so wonderful, darling. You feel so good. So good inside me. Oh Jesus, Arthur, Jesus and the God I don't believe in. If you keep this up I won't love you for anything else."

"Good enough reason. What the hell do you think I love you for?"

"For this. Of course for this. What else matters? For — now, honey, now. Be with me now, baby. After this there's nothing left."

"Yes now," he said. "Darling, I love you so."

"Yes," she said, "darling Arthur, lover, husband, God I love you, do it sweetheart, do it, do it NOW!"

Her screams echoed in the empty house where Fred had conceived her in silence, hopelessly upon the inert body of his dutiful wife, where they now exploded rapturously into the death which is the beginning of life. Can Fulvia die, Cleopatra had wondered contemptuously. Zelda could, and Arthur, and they lay together afterwards in a communion which encompassed the passion of their belonging.

"Dearest," she said at last, "much more of this and I won't be able to let you go at all. Not even for one night."

"I know," he said, beginning to move. "What do you think it does to me?"

"Stay here, damn you," she said, clutching his ass. "Your lousy cigarette can wait. So what are we going to do? It gets worse."

"Well," he said, sliding back until he was pressed hard against her and bending to kiss her breast, "I've got an idea or two."

"Your big ideas will be little pretty soon," she said. "What are we really going to do?"

"You'll have to let me have a cigarette if you're going to make me think."

"All right," she said, releasing him. "Ouch. You didn't have to do it like that, you know. Don't you ever think about how a girl feels?"

"All the time," he said, kissing the haven he had deserted. "Miss me?"

"Not when you're doing that. But it's no way to get a cigarette."

"Roger," he said lighting one for both of them. "Now what can I advise you on, Miss Huckaby?"

"The future, lover," she said, sitting up cross-legged with naked grace. "How much longer do you think we can play this game and get away with it?"

"Now how in hell," he said, reaching over to caress the damp bush she had opened to him, "do you expect me to think of anything but *now* when you sit like that?"

"Because that's what we're talking about, sweetie. That's your future you're making free with. Do you think we can keep on conning Vicki indefinitely? Don't stop."

"Why not, as long as we're careful? You know she's so damned set in that tight little world of hers it never occurs to her I might step out of it. She's got me all boxed and labelled, baby, and as long as I keep on looking that way she'll never guess a thing."

"Suppose some kind friend helps her get the idea?"

"Like who? Nobody knows but Captain Tom."

"Oh, darling," she said, leaning over to kiss him, "how can you be so naïve and still so wonderful? Look, you're coming alive again."

"What the hell did you expect, the way you're carrying on? Like who? Stay over here."

"Like Ulysses," she said, kneading him gently and laying her head on his shoulder, "that's like who."

"Now wait a minute," he said, "let's sit up here and talk sense for a minute. That's crazy, baby. Ulysses doesn't know a damned thing."

"Who said he knows anything? We're not talking about anything he has to prove. All he needs is to suspect."

"And you think he does?"

"Arthur, darling," she said, putting her hands on his shoulders, "do you have any idea how you look at me now? Don't you know your own town at all? They're born suspecting, baby, gossip's what they live on, and the looks you give and the way you touch me when you don't even realize it, that's enough to give Ulysses all the ideas he needs. The way you light a cigarette for me, honey, my God it's a sexual act and you don't even realize you never used to light them for me at all, do you think he's going to miss that?"

"So he sees it. I've been doing it for two months now and nothing's happened."

"Honey, you just don't understand peasants. Ulysses hasn't needed it yet. That's a dangerous game to play, and he won't take any risks he doesn't have to. How's the production battle coming?"

"Pretty good. We're almost up to our norm again. Next week we ought to pass it."

"Then we do have something to worry about. Shall I clue you?"

"Clue away."

"Then listen. And you'd better leave me alone if you want me to get this straight. If you do go ahead of the production figures next week, and I suspect you will the way you've been riding herd on them, here's what will happen. One morning when Vicki's alone in the house, she'll get an anonymous phone call. A woman's voice, a friend, calling to ask if she knows what's going on between you and me. A friend who believes in decency, and feels it's her duty to inform Vicki of what's happening right under her nose."

"A woman's voice?"

"Of course, stupid. So there'll be nothing to hang on Ulysses. What's Vicki going to do then?"

"Damn if I know. Laugh, maybe. She's too proud to go for that nonsense, and I really doubt she cares that much about me."

"Who's talking about you? We're talking about Vicki. It's exactly her pride that will be the hooker, lover, hurt pride about the husband she condescended to take into her bed who has the effrontery to make love to trash like me. The real hell of it will be that down deep she knows we're right in a way she's not, and she'll never forgive you for that. There'll be hell to pay, Art, believe me."

"Hell to pay with Vicki? She'd rather sneer."

"You don't know your ex-woman, baby. She'll scream so loud it'll blow this town apart."

"That's what Captain Tom said. That I didn't know her. Only he said she wouldn't scream."

"The night you stayed out, you mean? Same difference. That time she wasn't hurt, this time she will be."

"So you think she'll blow?"

"Jesus, baby why not? You mean she never blows up?"

"Oh, sometimes," he said, a vision of naked bumps and grinds floating uneasily before him, "but not often anymore, and it never lasts. She cools down in a little and wants to make up."

"You ever really put the screws on her?"

"No," he said thoughtfully. "No, I guess I haven't."

"In fact, when she starts to simmer, you back off, don't you?"

"Yes," he said, "I don't like the way it sounds, but I guess I do."

"Oh, honey," she said, kissing him quickly, "I don't mean to cross-examine you. That was you *then,* not now. What I'm trying to do is tell you what's likely to happen, and ask if you're really ready to face it. I don't want to get you into something you don't want. I'd rather we quit now while there's still time to patch it up. No matter how much it might hurt, I'd rather lose it now than live to realize you'd regretted it."

"Zelda," he said, cupping her chin to bring her eyes up to his, "one thing you can be sure of. I'll never regret us, darling. None of it. Not for a minute. God, dearest, you brought me to life. Do you think I could regret that?"

"Do you mean it, Arthur?" she said. "Are you sure you really mean it?"

Tears formed in pools on her eyelids and welled steadily down her cheeks. Her expression remained calm and unchanged, but the tears flowed evenly, so that already her cheeks were wet. She did not cry; the tears came, in quantities that astonished him, but except for a deeper intensity in her gaze, she showed no awareness of them.

"I mean it, darling," he said, sliding his cheek against her wet one. "I'll always mean it. Don't cry."

"Not crying," she said. "Just happy. How about when she blows up? Will you back down?"

"Never," he said. "Fuck her."

"Figuratively speaking?"

"Figuratively speaking."

"All the way up to the ceiling?"

"And over the roof."

"How about me?"

"Literally. Right down to the ground."

"Hell of a good idea," she said, starting to climb out of bed.

"Where do you think you're going?"

"Just trying to cooperate."

"Come on back, you silly bitch. It starts here."

"Oh," she said, her eyes sparkling behind the tears. "Yes, master."

And spread herself beside him.

14

The call came Wednesday at ten.

Vicki was sitting in the breakfast room, floating cream from a teaspoon onto her coffee. It was the marvelous idle hour which someone always interrupted. Arthur and the children were long gone; she had completed her own chores, which she performed as compulsively, and with equal annoyance to Katy, as she demanded her children execute those she imposed on them; and Katy, happily on her own at last, had begun the serious business of the day in the kitchen. The hours stretched ahead, meaningless but pleasant — a kind of peace that was all she had come to hope for. Trust the telephone to shatter it.

Marj Walker, she thought with annoyance as she rose reluctantly on the third ring and moved lazily toward the phone. Did she have to be such an eager beaver? Being an efficient chairman was one thing, but calling on Garden Club business every damned morning was something else. It would be almost easier if she did it herself again next time. Maybe she ought to think about it.

It was a strange voice.

"Mrs. Evans," it said, "you don't know me, or at least I hope you don't recognize me, because what I have to say isn't very pleasant. But we've talked it all over, a number of us, and we have decided someone has to tell you, and I'm elected to do it. Do you know about your husband and Zelda Huckaby, Mrs. Evans?"

"Who is this calling?"

"That doesn't matter. I only wanted —"

"It matters to me if someone calls and makes accusations about my own husband and isn't willing to identify herself."

"All right, Mrs. Evans, then I'll hang up. At least I've done my duty. If you don't want to be told, find out for yourself. Good-bye."

"Now who the hell would getting me up for a stupid game like that?" she wondered angrily as the line went dead. Instinctively she ranged herself with Arthur. Their private lives were off bounds for the sick minds that peddled hate anonymously by telephone because it was both easy and safe. If this woman had a party line she probably had a crony listening in to see how the high and mighty Mrs. Evans took it. Posing as a friend, practically. God, how did people get like that? You'd think they'd have more respect for themselves, if not for the people they were slandering. Impulsively, half way back to the table, she turned to call Arthur.

But between impulse and act the habits of years intervened. What had once been a natural gesture, in the days of their intimacy, would now be artificial and misleading. To call, now that she phoned only for occasional real crises or routine household chores, would put the whole thing out of focus. Inevitably, he would think it more important than she intended it to be. Which would, after all, only be playing into the hands of her tormentors. Better to tell him when he came home, when they could laugh at it over a drink.

But as the day wore on, small mice of doubt began gnawing at her certainty. *Why* had she called? It had been a woman, no doubt of that. The escape she had toyed with, the telephone games she remembered from her own childhood, simply would not do. She remembered every syllable. It was an adult, a reasonable adult. Pleasant. Even friendly.

There had been no hate in the voice. That was what she kept coming back to. Would the voice of a sick mind have been so calm, almost reluctant, speaking with the hesitation one felt when unpleasant things must be said for someone else's good? Even when she had practically insulted her, the woman had been friendly. Very well, Mrs. Evans, she had said, I won't bother you any more. I won't tell you what you don't want to hear. In a comparable situation, wasn't it exactly what she would have said herself?

Increasingly, she thought about Zelda. For Arthur to initiate a liaison was unthinkable. He couldn't, that's all. Perhaps she would think better of him if he could. But he couldn't. Especially now, when he had been more passionate and tender than in years, more loving in the way that once had been. But he could be led.

Why not? What did Zelda have to lose? For all the veneer

Fred had bought her, no one doubted what she was. Why else had she remained an old maid, in a town where eligible women married young? She had money, was attractive in a stylized if somewhat masculine way, and had been well schooled in appearing the lady she was not. But it hadn't sold, not in Phoenix, no matter what desperate and easily imaginable lengths she must have gone to. At thirty-five or thereabouts she was on the shelf. All the eligible men were married. What was left but married men? And who was handier than Art?

The role began to come alive inside her, Vicki becoming Zelda in a way that excited and terrified her, seeing her husband through the eyes of the predator, Arthur reborn in the red haze of concupiscence, herself a grey figure in the background, carelessly sketched in tones of habit and indifference. In this reconstructed universe, she realized, Vicki had not even the reality of an obstacle. Only in the next act, when an antithesis was demanded for synthesis, would she come alive in order to be overborne.

She was in the kitchen when Arthur arrived, kissed him with their new affection, poured Katy's drink herself, and suggested they have their cocktail hour upstairs in his study alone. Relaxed together on the couch, she broke the precedent of years by asking him about work, unlistened attentively while he explained the production situation, and then moved on to the heart of the present matter.

"Darling," she said casually, "how's Zelda these days?"

"Why, the same as ever, I guess," Arthur said warily. "Why do you ask?"

"No special reason. I just got to thinking about her today and wondered why we never have her over. She's such a nice girl I think we ought to sometime."

"We've never had her over because you've never asked her," he said, bitterness edging his voice. "I guess she's not good enough for the crowd of pinheads we cultivate."

"Why, Arthur," Vicki said sweetly, turning to look at him with hard eyes, "I didn't know you cared so much. We'd have had her over long ago if you'd only said so."

"It's not that," he said too loudly. To his horror, a muscle behind his thumb began to twitch violently, and he put his glass down before Vicki noticed. "It just makes me mad for a nice girl like Zelda to be ostracized because her father came from across the tracks."

"Ostracized?" Vicki said dangerously. "I don't know what you mean. She belongs to the country club. She never lacks for dates, from what I hear, and she goes to all the big parties. I've never thought we had an obligation to include her in our own set."

"You're the one suggested we invite her over."

"That proves my point. But why this sudden interest on your part? I never heard you talk like this before."

"It's not sudden. You just never asked me before. In fact, I don't know when's the last time you asked my opinion on anything."

"That's not fair, Arthur. I'll admit we don't seem as close as we used to, but that's marriage, I guess, and you can't blame it all on me. We do better than most people we know."

They sat quietly, their heads still above waters into which neither of them had planned to venture. There was a current between them, a waiting and a knowledge that another word would tumble them into depths from which there might be no returning. Arthur desperately wanted a drink, but the first tentative move of his hand from his sheltering leg told him he could never lift his glass. Falsely quiet, he stared hopelessly at nothing and waited for Vicki to take the plunge Zelda's wisdom told him she could not avoid.

"Let's not play games, Arthur," she said at last. "You know what I'm talking about. Someone called me today and told me about you and Zelda. I didn't believe them then, but now I know it's true. It is true, isn't it? There's no point lying about it now."

So it was here. Anger and a kind of peace steadied his hand, and he lifted his glass and took a long sip before answering.

"Who called?" he asked quietly.

"What does it matter? Some woman I don't know. She just thought I ought to know what's going on."

"It matters a good deal. There's nothing between Zelda and me, if you want to know, but I've been expecting you to get a call like this."

"I don't understand."

"I'll try to explain. But let me fix us a drink first."

99

The tension between them remained while he filled their glasses with his old sureness, but its focus had shifted. Beneath the calm which misled them both, Arthur was filled with a wild joy. His first real lie to Vicki had gone off, unintentionally almost, with an ease that astonished him. He had the upper hand now, and they both knew it. When he handed her the glass, Vicki, poised catlike in her murderous femininity but thrown back on uncertainty by this new tack, looked at him with her old directness.

"All right," she said, "explain."

"It's simple enough," he said, lifting his glass. "Your health. Remember what I was telling you about the production situation?"

"Production?"

"A few minutes ago. Right here. You asked me, for God's sake, how I was coming with Ulysses, and I told you. What's the point trying to tell you anything if you don't listen?"

"Of course," she lied, remembering nothing. "I'm sorry, darling. I had my gears shifted."

"Then keep them where they are now," he said with his old grin, feeding his new confidence on this further small uncertainty, "and listen. Ulysses is the whole point, you see? Remember the night I stayed over at Captain Tom's and you got so mad at me?"

"I didn't get mad once you all explained it to me. I was very good about it."

"Yes, you were, darling," he said, putting his hand on her knee. Desire suddenly stirred in his loins, and while his mind framed the next stage of his lie, the strategy of eternal commitment to Zelda, his hand moved of its own volition beneath her dress, separating the legs that fell gently apart for him, between her soft thighs to the waiting hairy softness.

"Jesus," he said as his fingers entered her. "No pants."

"You know I always think ahead," she said, lifting her face to him as he shifted himself, put his other arm behind her, and bent to kiss her. "But you were saying?"

"I was saying this," he said, burying his tongue and fingers in her, all of her opening to him until they fell back awkwardly on the couch.

100

"Oh, darling," she said thickly, her eyes blurred with passion, "lock the goddamn door and come back here. Quick."

They were together, her trim dress knotted wildly around her waist, his pants tossed heedlessly across the ice bucket, mouth, for the first time in years, to mouth, soul almost to soul. In their ecstacy, a violence which swept them back to the stars, her eyes locked his and their mouths were joined in the union they had forgotten. Even afterwards, as they lay satiate in their half-clothed embrace, she rubbed her cheek softly against his and whispered gently in his ear.

"Darling," she said, "that was wonderful, wonderful. Was it good for you?"

"Wonderful," he said truthfully, lost in fulfillment. "Marvelous, Vicki. Like it used to be."

"And there's nothing between you and that woman, is there, darling?"

"Nothing," he lied easily, freed, in this moment, from guilt either to her or to Zelda. "There's nothing, baby. I'll explain it when we get up."

"You don't have to," she said. "I get the picture. Ulysses is trying to blackmail you because you're winning out?"

"That's it. Captain Tom warned me about it that night, but I didn't really believe it. But after watching Ulysses for a month, I realize he'd do anything, so I wasn't surprised when you told me about the call."

"What a cheap, poor white trick. And what insolence, thinking he could use me like that. You ought to fire him tomorrow."

"I can't fire him for that, honey. Not now. He's doing the job because I'm making him do it. But when this doesn't work, he'll try sabotage. And I will fire him for that. And he knows."

"Then let him hang himself, darling. I'll help. I'll —"

Her snores began, soft at first, and her head fell slackly away toward the coffee table, her open mouth coming to rest a foot from her untouched drink. Gently, he eased himself out of her, put on his pants, and sat down with his glass in the arm chair opposite. Snoring, disheveled, her dress now tight under her armpits, capped by the brassiere he had somehow freed to reach her breasts, her legs still spread for love, her wet crotch oozing on the slip cover she kept immaculate — she was more beautiful

101

than he had seen her in years, and he looked at her with compassion and a kind of love.

And with certainty. How could it be, he wondered, that out of passion which was almost the communion that had first joined them, he could know irrevocably that they must part, and that he must be with Zelda forever? He'd have to tell Zelda about tonight, of course, and probably she wouldn't understand. Well, she'd have to learn. Understanding was a part of the price for their future, the kind of knowledge, perhaps even wisdom, into which life was suddenly thrusting him. The love he had felt tonight for Vicki was good. It would be lost, probably, in the bitterness of parting, but they were both better for the fact that, however briefly, it had existed once again.

Except for the lie that had made it possible. The lies must end. She deserved better, and so did he. And so did Zelda. Perhaps Zelda was wrong after all, and tonight would free them to deal honestly with a reality they must all face, free him and Vicki to part with affection, and sanity, and such love as would always remain, to work together for the children who would be their mutual charge and bond.

Perhaps. He refilled his glass and sat quietly for half an hour, brooding peacefully, to the accompaniment of Vicki's snores, on the shape of things to come until a great crash against the door summoned him back to reality.

"Hey Dad," Hank's voice came impatiently, "open up, willya? Katy's all ready with dinner. Whatta you doing in there with the door locked? I banged my head when I tried to open it."

"Then you should have come to a stop before you tried the knob," Arthur said cheerfully. "I'm working and your mother is sleeping on the couch. Now you go down and tell Katy dinner will be served in fifteen minutes."

"Fifteen *minutes?* Cripes, Dad, that's all night. I'm starving."

"Then tell her half an hour. I'd like another drink anyway."

"*Okay,* okay. I'll tell her fifteen minutes. I sure don't want to sit around starving while you two souse it up. But what's she sleeping for? She had a nap this afternoon. And how come you had the door locked?"

"So you wouldn't come roaring in here and wake her up. Now beat it, young man, and give Katy the message or maybe you'll never eat."

"Okay."

He was gone in an avalanche of feet down the stairs, culminating in a leap from the bottom landing that shook the house. Smiling, Arthur rose, kissed Vicki gently between her legs, put his tongue in her navel, and kissed her on the mouth until her eyes opened and she stared at him blankly.

"Wha?" she said.

"Time to wake up, darling," he said. "Our young man was just up to tell us dinner is ready."

"My God, he didn't see me like this, did he?"

"Don't worry. The door was locked. I told him dinner in fifteen minutes. You remember how you got this way?"

"It's beginning to come back. God, look what I've done to the couch."

"So?"

"So turn the cushion over until I can work on it after supper, will you? Hank's liable to come up here sniffing around for evidence. He's getting to be the age."

"Sniffing is the word. You want your drink freshened?"

"Damn right, since you knocked me out and deprived me of it. How many've you had since you had your way with me?"

"One."

"Then have another, lover, while I get dressed. You earned it. Be with you in ten minutes."

She kissed him lightly and ran across the hall. Thoughtfully, he mixed new drinks, wondering if perhaps it might have been.

15

"I understand, dearest," Zelda said. "At least I think I do. I did something almost like it once, with a man I'd told good-bye because he was really interested in somebody else, and then we got drunk and went to bed together. Only it's not the same, is it? I was ashamed of that, and you're not. You're glad for the love because you'd like it not to end in bitterness. Is that it? I think I understand that."

"That's it," Arthur said, sitting up in bed. "I want it for the children —"

"And for yourself."

"Yes, for myself. And for Vicki, and for you too. What good is bitterness doing anybody? It only destroys. One of the things I've learned from you, baby, whether you realize it or not, is never to be ashamed of love. I'd like whatever love and friend-ship there is to be. My commitment, that's all for you —"

"You can't be committed to me in bed with her."

"I know that, baby. That's why I can't keep this up. That's why we've got to end it, why the lies have to stop. The lies are what I can't stand. They make me feel dirty. I want to tell her the truth, honey, but I can't unless you say so. Are you ready?"

"Darling Arthur, you know I'm ready. I have been from the beginning. Ready for anything. But I want you only when you're free inside yourself, ready for us, for whatever we must do, because it's what you want yourself. You can't be my man, darling, until you're your own. I'd rather never have you do anything just because you think I want it. That's why I could never push you."

"So now I don't need pushing. You still think things will blow up?"

"I'd lie to you if I said I didn't."

"I've been thinking maybe Vicki and I having been closer would make it easier for her to understand. More ready to ac-cept me for what I have to be."

"Or harder for her. You've made her more aware of what she's losing. You're not a woman, lover, and you overlook one thing."

"What's that?"

"That night you've been telling me about. It made you feel good. Did it ever occur to you that, once you tell her, it might make Vicki feel dirty?"

"May be," he said, lifting her up and holding her close. "There's nothing I can do about that now. Kiss me, darling, quietly, and then I've got to go. I want to be home when she gets back, and sit down soberly and tell her the truth. Whatever happens will happen, that's all. I've got to do what I have to."

They kissed, tenderly while Vicki maneuvered adroitly from the floor at a Garden Club meeting, ruthlessly, having determined that Marj must go, promoting confusion under the guise of seeming cooperation. The session ended in turmoil, an impasse which was resolved by Vicki's being drafted as a member of an *ad hoc* committee to restudy plans for this summer's show and report back at the next meeting. Well pleased, she drove home quickly and efficiently, eager to share her success with Arthur.

Share. She meant it, almost, she thought as she negotiated Phoenix's quiet streets; at least for the first time in years she could act as if she did. The week since the call had left things where they had brought them that evening. Arthur had been attentive and loving, staying home evenings to work in his study and coming to bed early to make love. They had never again reached the union that had betrayed them on the couch, but it was passionate and intense, and closer than it had been for more years than either liked to remember. There had been no more calls.

And inside? Vicki refused to look. The doubt was there, entangled with a fear she had never thought to feel, a sense of what it might mean if the man whom she had taken for granted so long, the husband whom she was accustomed to consider hers by right, should suddenly wrench himself loose. For the first time since the early days of their marriage, she looked outside herself at their relationship and realized that despite her long withdrawal, despite her feeling of empty self-sufficiency, her life

105

was as inextricably joined to Arthur's as in the time of their most passionate union. He was still at the core of her universe — dutiful, useful, but *necessary,* the axis round which her own careful unreality revolved. The chilling fact was that she had to have him, and if that bitch thought she could steal him, she'd damn well find out what kind of buzz saw she'd stuck her paw in.

Anger boiled in her, a blind flash of pure hatred so intense that she pulled the car to the curb a block from the house. It would never do to arrive like this. She lighted a cigarette and noticed with shame that her hands were trembling. Damn. Much more of this and she'd be back on phenobarb even though she hadn't taken a sleeping pill for a week. Arthur had seen to that, bless him, and now she was being a fool again. It couldn't be true when they made such glorious love. Arthur wasn't built that way, all his romantic notions about communion made it impossible. She had no doubts at night, lying close together after love or waking in the morning, tender and close. Maybe there was more to be said for communion than she'd let herself admit.

But the days were plain hell. Alone, with nothing to sustain her except an empty house and a meaningless life, Arthur with his marvelous cock gone to work with that bitch and his silly quarrel with Ulysses, the children enmeshed in a life to which she would soon release them entirely — what was her protection then against the doubts that tormented her, the voices inside her head which at any moment might pick up the phone and give her chapter and verse? There was none. Only herself, and this sneak attack at the point where she needed no defenses had taught her how frail her carefully wrought security would prove to be.

"Now that'll do, Vicki," she told herself, taking a last drag on her cigarette and flicking it crisply out the window. "You've gotten through another day and there's a whole night ahead of you. Now why don't you quit acting like a jackass and go back and enjoy it?"

Desire warmed her, lust for the darkness in which she would drown herself, and she started the car and rolled gently home. Arthur's car was still parked in the driveway, she noted with unconscious relief, pulled carefully to the left to make room for her. With a sudden flood of happiness, she stopped precisely

106

beside his car, ran lightly up the walk, and let herself into the darkened hall.

"Darling," she called in the black silence, "are you upstairs?"

"In the study," his grey voice answered, muffled by his retreat but speaking straight to her heart. "Come on up. I've got a nightcap for us."

As she started up the stairs, the phone rang.

"I'll get it down here," she called, snapping on the light with a gesture that had once been automatic. Marj again probably, calling to apologize. To apologize, the stupid fool, not even realizing what she'd done to her. It couldn't happen to a nicer girl.

"Mrs. Evans," the voice said, "while you were at your meeting your husband was with Zelda Huckaby. His car was parked in front of her house until fifteen minutes ago."

The line went dead before she could answer, leaving her standing blankly, the phone lifeless in her hand. She felt nothing. It was as if, in the moment she had known must come, all the lights had gone out inside her, leaving only an emptiness in which nothing, neither love nor hate, the joys she had hoarded nor the pain she feared, could endure. An arctic night of the soul, blue-dark and absolute. And incredibly lonely. An aloneness such as she had never experienced, locked now, suddenly and forever, in the frozen wastes of self.

Might as well get it over, she thought listlessly. Not that it really mattered. At least she could listen to his lies while she decided what to do.

He was pouring their drinks when she came quietly into the study.

"Ready and waiting," he said, handing her a glass. "Jesus, you look like you need it. Was the meeting as rough as that?"

"Kind of," she said. "I had to put Marj in her place. I'm tired."

"Who was on the phone?"

"Nobody. Wrong number, I guess. They hung up."

"You feel awake enough to talk?"

"I can listen."

"That'll do. There's something I've got to tell you, Vicki."

"Yes?"

"I lied to you about Zelda. There is something between us. I love her, and I want to marry her."

"You *what?* Marry her? Oh, Arthur, you can't mean that."

The glacier inside her split wide, and she tumbled into a great fissure of self-pity, falling free again into an exquisite sadness. Her face crumpled, and welcome tears misted her eyes. A great love welled in her heart, compassion for them both, for this delusion that was so maddeningly, endearingly like him, and hope in the knowledge that this aberration too would pass. Marry her? My God, were there no lengths to which this sickness of middle age would not carry men? No irrationality which their pathetic search for their lost youth could not justify? Relief swelled in her, mingling deliciously with her sadness. Thank God. She hadn't realized that Zelda was also a fool.

"Don't cry, honey," Arthur said, reaching across to put his hand on her shoulder. "I'm sorry it has to be this way, you don't know how sorry. But it is, and that's how it has to be."

"Not crying exactly," she said, taking his hand in hers and pressing it to her lips. "I don't know whether to laugh or cry. Darling, don't you realize how insane you're being? Don't you know it's infatuation you're talking about, not love? You and Zelda married? My God, Arthur, have you ever really stopped to look at it? You know what she is, where she came from. The whole town knows. If you were infatuated with somebody that made sense for you, a woman, not a thing like her, then I'd feel different probably, madly jealous and terrified of losing you. But surely, darling, surely you don't expect me to take this seriously. Just think about yourself, Arthur. Forget me, and the children, your job and responsibilities and position, everything but yourself. Don't you know if I let you go tonight you'd be back in a month? Telling me how wrong you were and how much you need me? Begging me to start over again? Can't you understand that, honey? Don't you even know what kind of person you are? And what she is?"

"She's the best woman I ever knew, and the finest person. She's taught me what life is all about."

"The best woman? That poor white slut? That pretentious little bitch with her phony clothes and accent, acting as if she were somebody instead of the piece of trash everybody knows she is? At least her father had the good sense not to pretend to be anything except what he was. He was a good man even if he was a Cracker. He knew his place and he didn't try to step out of it, and the town respected him for it. But this thing. Jesus, Arthur, don't you see why she wants you? She's a social climber, a cheap little *nouvea riche* bitch. All you are is a way up for her, darling, can't you understand that? She'll squeeze you like an orange and throw you away when she's ready for a younger man. She's on the make, Arthur. My God, do I have to draw a picture for you?"

"Zelda isn't on the make for anything. She doesn't want position. She *is*. All she wants to be."

"And I suppose that's why she didn't get married all these years. Waiting until she could *be* with you, with your brains and beauty and one of the best names in town. Oh, Arthur, are you an utter fool? Don't you know she didn't get married because nobody would have her? Because everybody saw through her until you came along, middle aged and ready to fall for any younger woman who'd make you feel young again. Any phony who'd butter you up to get what she wants. I'll bet she butters your cock before she sucks it."

"You don't have to be disgusting, Vicki," he said. "You're the one's always telling me profanity is a sign of a limited mind."

"Disgusting, my ass," she said, anger suddenly possessing her; a demon took control of her voice and will, "you're the one that's disgusting. Making love to me like I was the whole world, lying not just with words but with all of you, and then going off to screw around with that cheap whore. Right here on this goddamn couch the night I got that first call and you lied to me, lied to me with your cock in me after you made love to me and told me how wonderful it was. You and your big fat words about communion and love. Jesus, Arthur, you don't know what love is. How disgusting can you get? Honesty you talk about, you goddamn liar. When was the last time you were with her? Of course you'll lie about that too."

"I won't lie to you any more, Vicki," he said quietly. "I only lied to you because I didn't have the right to expose somebody else. Now we've talked about it, and neither of us want any more lies. I was with her tonight."

"You mean while I was at my meeting you were fucking that thing?"

109

"We made love, yes."

Deliberately, the demon steadying her hand, she threw her drink in his face. When she lifted her arm to throw the glass, he caught her wrist. With her free hand she clutched at his balls, and when he had secured that wrist, she lifted her feet and drove them savagely into his groin. Maddened, his thigh bruised by her heels despite her bad aim, he pushed her savagely back on the couch, sat on her legs, and pushed her wrist into her mouth. Her wild eyes glared at him.

"I ought to break your neck, you crazy bitch," he said, "but I won't. But I'll hold you like this all night until you're ready to quit this nonsense. You understand?"

Slowly, the madness went out of her eyes. When the tears began, she nodded her head, and he lifted her wrist from her mouth.

"Ready to quit?" he said.

"I'm through," she said hoarsely. "I'm sorry, Arthur. I didn't know I could act like that. I'm all right now."

He released her and she sat up, sobbing quietly.

"If I give you another drink," he said, "will you not throw it? I promise you, I'll pour the goddamn ice bucket on you if you do."

"I won't throw it. Only make it strong. What I hit you with was mostly water."

They sat drinking quietly, lost in their private worlds, until she looked up with a sudden smile.

"You'll have to admit my aim was good," she said. "I didn't waste a drop."

The simple humanity broke him, and he gave himself over to the great sobs that racked him, burying his face in his hands while his tears mingled with the liquor he had not bothered to wipe away.

"Oh, baby," she said, coming over to sit on his lap and cradling his head in her arms, "don't cry, dearest, please don't cry. I'm sorry I acted like that, Arthur, I won't any more. Only you don't know what you do to me. In bed with that bitch while I thought you were home waiting to make love to me, coming home with her stink on you to take me in your arms. What do you expect a woman to do who loves you, Arthur? How would you like it if you were me?"

110

"I'd hate it, I guess," he said, "but I wouldn't act like that. What I came home for tonight was to tell you the truth, Vicki. But that's not what breaks my heart. It's the bitterness and hate. Jesus, can't we admit that we're finished without ripping at each other's guts? You call it love. Is it love when you try to smash my balls?"

"But I was crazy jealous, Arthur. Out of my mind. Don't you know jealousy is a part of love? If you really loved her, maybe I'd be different. If she were good enough for you, I'd say all right, that's how it has to be. But you don't love her. You're infatuated with her maybe, though God knows why, but you love me. I've lived with you nineteen years, Arthur. Don't you think I know you by now? I know from the way you make love to me. You couldn't do that and love somebody else. You're not built that way."

"No, I'm not," he said, "and it's tearing me apart. Of course I love you in a way, Vicki. I hope I always do. When I make love to you I mean it, but it's only with part of me. I don't love you any more in the way you think, and I never will. As for knowing me, no, you don't know me at all. We haven't communicated for years, and we're not communicating now. You won't like this, but it's because Zelda does understand me, because we do communicate, that I can give part of myself to you. I don't suppose that makes any sense to you."

"You can say that again," she said, her old contempt rising in her. She got off his lap, drained her glass, and sat down on the couch. "I want another drink. No, your big words don't mean anything to me, Arthur. They never have. And they don't to you. What you're really talking about is a way to have your cake and eat it too. To have me and still mess around with your poor white whore. Communion. That's just a fancy word for a new piece of ass. A cheap one too, that anyone in town could have that'd take the trouble. Only most decent men are too smart to want to. Except old high-thinking, fancy-talking Arthur, who's sucker enough to let a cheap little bitch take him in a town that knows her like this one does. Gimme my drink."

"Here we go again," he said wearily, handing her the glass. "You're going to be drunk after that one, and then we *will* be at it again. But Jesus, Vicki, can't you talk about people without being so damned full of hate? Don't you realize how you cheapen yourself? It's nobody else you dirty. It's you."

"Don't worry about me, buster," she said, downing half her glass. "I'll stay clean. I've got too much self-respect to dirty myself the way you do. Worry about yourself when you're in bed with that two-bit whore. But I'll make a deal with you. You think you have to have her? You need to find out what she's really like? Okay, go ahead. Only be a little more careful about it, will you, so's the whole town doesn't know about it any more than they have to. Not that they don't already. That call, in case you're interested, was somebody calling to tell me your car was parked at Zelda's house. I spose that's what scared you into coming clean. So go ahead. Just don't come home without taking a shower, and don't crawl into bed with me until you've scrubbed with good strong soap. Okay? I want a nightcap."

"Pour it yourself," he said, "you're on your own. Do you realize how disgusting you're being, Vicki?"

"Don't be stupid," she said, taking the bottle. "Damn right I'll pour it. Got a husband wants to make a jackass out of himself, okay, give him enough rope to hang himself. Damn fool will learn and come crawling back to momma soon enough. Then maybe she'll take him back. Maybe not. Wait and see. Keep the goddamn dirt out of the house, though. Don't come back here without a bath."

"Go to bed, Vicki," he said. "You're drunk."

"Goin'," she said. "But my own way. Cause *I* want to. Finish this drink, then gonna take two sleeping pills. Two. This conversation bores me, and I need my rest. Be quiet when you come to bed, buster, and be sure you scrub clean. I might want to use you before morning. If I feel like it when I wake up, I just might show you what a piece of ass is really like. So long, sucker."

She emptied her glass, gave him a brilliant smile, and staggered out.

For long minutes he sat quietly, sipping his drink while he tried to put all his Vickis into one. It was no use. Where had they come from, this series of women, loving, hating, cajoling, malevolent, dry-eyed and weeping, sober, drunk, murderously tender, coldly passionate — fragmentations of the one woman, presumably, with whom he had lived for almost twenty years? Things will explode, Zelda had said. He no longer knew what to expect. He no longer knew whom he was dealing with. Only that these protean women, this infinite circle of masks, might proliferate endlessly, and that as he felt his way cautiously around the ring that hemmed him, there was no spot that roughened into reality, no firmness he could grasp to bull his way through to freedom.

What to do? *Run,* the life inside him shouted, blow your nose and go before it's too late. But his will would not listen. The goddamned irrationality couldn't last forever. At some point, if they stood steadfast, the shrewd practicality which was the core of Vicki's being would reassert itself, she would collect herself into a single person, and they would make whatever arrangements were best for all concerned. He could leave his job honorably, do whatever he could for his children, maintain a semblance of friendliness with Vicki, and depart with Zelda into a life it almost frightened him to contemplate.

But meanwhile. Meanwhile it's going to be rough, Arthur boy, he thought, rougher than either of us imagined. So you asked for it, buddy. You made your bed, and it's up to you to lie in it. But not till those goddamn pills work. With all that liquor they ought to knock her out for the night, and one performance of that show is about all you can take. A nightcap is in order, son, taken slow and easy and then into the sack. No matter what kind of hell she dreams up in the morning, your war with Ulysses is still on, and from the looks of the weather around here you'd better grab all the sleep you can get.

He drank, and toasted Zelda in his heart.

He surfaced at three-thirty, climbing up from an abyss of sleep to feel her mouth and hands on him, her bush tight against his lips while his body tingled with the pleasure she was skillfully unleashing. Half conscious, he responded avidly, kissing the warmth that would soon envelop him totally. What life was about. Being, and loving, and—

Abruptly, he was awake. Instinctively, with a single violent motion, he thrust his hands into her belly and pushed her roughly aside.

"Don't," she said thickly, straining against him. "Lemme back. Gotta."

113

"No goddamn it," he said, shoving her away again and sitting up. "No. For Christ's sake, Vicki, be sensible."

"Don't wanta be sensible. Wanta make love."

"After last night? Love?"

"Who cares about last night? Love you. Want you now."

"You remember what happened? How you went to bed?"

"Sure I remember. So what? You're here now. In bed with me. Come on."

Her hands were on him, and he swung his legs sidewise and sat on the edge of the bed.

"I didn't take a bath."

"Don't give a damn. Just said that to be nasty. Don't hurt me any more, Arthur. I need you now."

Once again, the humanness unmanned him, and he turned and laid his hand on her breast.

"I don't want to hurt you, darling," he said. "But I can't make love to you now. Out of hate, and bitterness, and desperation? Not now, Vicki, especially not now when we've come this far. It has to be for love."

"Love," she said bitterly. "Who the hell knows what love is? Was it love when you gave me a lie, fulfilled me with what I thought was truth when you were just pretending?"

"I wasn't pretending. I meant it, though maybe not the way you thought. But anyway, you're just talking now, Vicki. You didn't give a damn what I meant or didn't. You just wanted the physical act. It could have been anybody."

"That's not true, and you know it. I never wanted anybody but you. Nobody else has laid a hand on me since the first time you made love to me."

"I believe you. But that's not what I was talking about. You just wanted sex. My body was all that mattered to you. My prick, to use the word you don't like."

"I don't mind the word," she said, sitting up. "Get us a cigarette, will you? I've got quite a vocabulary, Arthur, believe me. I just put it aside after we were married. Trying to make myself into something different, I guess. But for the right reasons. The wife and mother we both decided to make me. I'd been around plenty before I met you, you know."

"I always figured you had."

"All right, I had. But Jesus, Arthur, that was a long time

114

ago. I was a kid then. I wanted to be alive, not just drift into the stuffy world my parents thought was living, and sex was the way out. Especially after I found I loved it. Where's that damned cigarette?"

He snapped on the light, found the package, and lit up for them both. As he turned to hand her one, he saw that she was sitting cross-legged like Zelda, unselfconscious and beautiful in her nakedness. Releasing the cigarette, he turned out the light and locked his hand between his legs, hiding even in the darkness the life he knew he could not deny.

"Why didn't you ever talk to me like this before, Vicki?" he asked.

"What for? You'd only have thought I was cheap. Well, maybe I was. But I had to be then. I'm not ashamed of it."

"But don't you know that's what I loved you for? The wildness? Do you think we'd ever have gotten married if we hadn't started that way, that night in the car?"

"It brought us together, sure. Christ, have I ever underestimated sex? But marriage, that's something else, Arthur. You change when you're married. You have to. You take on responsibilities, position, obligations to yourself and other people. It's all right to be a wild kid. Maybe it's even good. But not a wild wife and mother. You didn't marry me for that."

"Not that way, Vicki, no. Not with other people. But wild together, true to the life in ourselves. Sure we take on responsibilities, but we shouldn't give up ourselves. That's the mistake I made, I've finally realized. The one you made too."

"Arthur, won't you ever grow up? We didn't make any mistakes. We did what we had to. You became a responsible man, a successful one, and I've been proud of you. I tried to be a good wife and mother, and I think I have been. You lose something, sure, but that's what happens when you get older. We're not kids anymore. I'm forty and you're forty-two, and we have to act like it. Our trouble is you still think you're twenty-one, and free to whore around any time you want to."

"With Zelda, I presume you mean from your choice of language."

"Yes, with that bitch. I did things that stupid before I met you, Arthur. I'm not proud of them, but I did. But God, that

115

was then. I couldn't do them now. I've grown up, thank God, and I've learned the difference between right and wrong."

"Which is?"

"Among other things, the difference is that you don't go being unfaithful with the town whore, and even if you're that stupid you don't talk about leaving your wife and children for her."

"Goddam it, Vicki," he said, lighting another cigarette in the dark, "can't we talk without your starting to call Zelda names?"

"I'll take that one," she said, her full breast lighting in the matchlight as she stretched out her hand. "So I insulted your beautiful pure darling again. I'm sorry. I didn't mean to hurt your feelings. But the point's the same. You're a man now, Arthur. Isn't it time you stopped acting like a child?"

"And quit looking for love and fulfillment, you mean, like an old man of forty-two should?"

"Oh, Jesus, Arthur," she said with a harsh laugh, "are we back here again? Sometimes I think you got inoculated with big words. I'm your love, Arthur. Your marriage is your fulfillment. Your children, your job, your place in the community. You've got more than any man I know."

"In your terms, maybe. That's all you can think about. But not in mine."

"No, not in your terms," she mimicked, "not in sweet-talking, romantic Arthur's. Next thing you know we'll be talking about communion again."

"Damn right we will," he said, turning away from her while he lit his own cigarette, "that's what we started with before we got sidetracked on all this nonsense. It's what I need, what I have to have, what I haven't had with you since the day we began to have children. And what I won't live without any longer."

"And you'll get it with *her*?" she said contemptuously. "Listen, Arthur. I won't try to tell you any more about Huckaby. What you won't listen to, you'll have to find out for yourself. But I want to say something to you about yourself. Now it's the children's fault. That's a new one. God, aren't you ever going to realize that the trouble is in yourself? You think I object to words like *prick*. I don't, though I prefer *cock*, if you must know. The ones I do object to are the big ones you use instead

116

of living. Instead of being a man. *Communion.* You're right, we haven't had it. And you know why? Because you haven't had the guts to make me into the woman I ought to be. You've let me boss you, push you around, been sweet to me when you should have kicked me in the ass, wanted me to give you love instead of forcing me to love you whether I wanted to or not. A real man would have had me eating out of his hand. But not you. No, by God, you have to have it mutual, nice and gooey and tender. Communion, you call it. Shit, Arthur, a real woman doesn't want your kind of communion. She wants to be dominated, dragged by the hair, forced to be something different from the silly bitch she'll become by herself. She wants to be *raped.*"

Abruptly, she slid to her side of the bed, turned on the light, and disappeared through the door. She was back almost instantly, bearing the bottle and two glasses.

"Might as well toast on that one," she said, sitting beside him. "I never expected to say that to you, but you asked for it. Now do you understand why I can't turn you loose with a man-eater like Huckaby? When?"

"When," he said, taking the glass. "Look, Vicki, I'm glad you said it. There's truth in it, too much. I haven't been man enough most of our marriage, and I have let you call the tune. The reasons were right, but it doesn't make me any less wrong. What you don't understand is that I *am* a man now, and I know what I want. It isn't you, baby, or anybody like you. You want to be raped because you don't like what you are. You want a man who has the contempt for you that you feel for yourself, someone who'll make you what you can't make yourself. I don't want that. I want a real woman, a loving one, not your hating kind, who wants communion because she likes herself the same way she does me, whom I'll dominate but only half a step ahead, who's her own woman all the time she's also mine. That's what I want, Vicki, and that's why I've got to have Zelda."

"Oh, baby," she said, draining her glass and putting it on the floor beside her, "won't you ever understand? Don't you think I'm glad you're a man? Don't you know I feel it, or I'd never have said what I did? But don't you know I'm your woman too? Look at me Arthur. Look at me," she said, putting his hands on her breasts, "aren't I beautiful? Aren't I all the woman you could want?"

117

"Yes, you're beautiful, Vicki," he said, feeling her nipples rise beneath his fingers. "You always have been."

"And aren't I good in bed, baby? Aren't I wonderful to make love to? Don't I know how to make you happy? Feel that," she said, shifting his left hand, "all moist and warm and waiting for you. Doesn't that make you want me? Doesn't that make you know I'm your woman?"

"Yes, it makes me want you, Vicki," he said. "You know that."

"Then take me, darling," she said, her hand alive on him, "take me now and let's be togther and start everything over. Let's forget all this, honey, and be glad for what we learned from it and begin the life we should have had all along. Kiss me, Arthur, and then let me kiss you."

"No, Vicki," he said, holding her off, "we're not going to make love. I want you, yes, but only to say goodbye, not to pretend we're beginning anything new. We're through, baby, and that's where we have to start from now on."

"Oh, for Christ's sake, Arthur," she said, picking up his glass, "what the hell have you let that bitch do to you? You're a man still, I can feel that, but Jesus, have you forgotten what to do with it? What are you, her eunuch now?"

"Just her man, Vicki."

"Then get the hell out of my bed," she said, pushing him off balance so that he fell awkardly to the floor, "get your miniscule cock out of here and leave me alone."

She drummed him with her feet, kicking wildly at his face and groin until he disentangled himself and threw her legs back on the bed. When he came after her, she bit the hand with which he gripped her mouth. The pain was excruciating, and for the first time he struck her, beating her across the head with his open palm until she opened her mouth to scream. Both hands freed, he locked them around her throat, seeing the blood and banging her head against the bedstead.

"Don't kill me," she gasped, her eyes bright with terror, "don't, Arthur, please, please don't."

Her voice cut through the red mist, and he lowered her head to the pillow, easing his grip but still holding her fast.

"All right," he said hoarsely, choking on his own acrid breath, "I won't. I should, but I won't. But get this straight,

118

you bitch. You've done that for the last time, understand? Another time and I'll break your goddamn neck. I'm going to sleep in the study now, to try to get some sleep for tomorrow. We've had it for tonight. You understand?"

"Just go away," she sobbed, averting her face. "Leave me alone, please. I won't bother you. Just leave me alone."

He freed her and went to the bathroom to examine his hand. Only a flesh wound, but the marks of her small teeth made a semicircle behind his thumb. A good enough symbol to end on, he thought, picked up a pillow and sheet, locked the study door, and settled himself on the couch. He was asleep almost immediately, falling into a darkness dreamless and profound.

When he waked, her voice filtering through at last, the study was grey with morning light.

"Arthur," she called, rattling the door, "wake up, Arthur, and let me in. I've got to talk to you."

"For Christ's sake, Vicki," he said, "I told you to let me alone. What time is it?"

"Five o'clock. Please, Arthur, I'm not going to make a scene. I've got to talk to you before the children wake up."

"All right," he said, getting up and putting on his robe. "I guess I'm awake for good anyway. But I warn you, no games."

"No games," she said. "I promise. Please open up."

She came in quietly and sat demurely on the edge of the couch. She had put on a high-necked negligee, he noted with relief, and fixed her face and hair. It was only when he sat down beside her that he caught her fragrance.

"Jesus, Vicki," he said, "you smell like a goddamn barroom."

"Ought to," she said. "Been drinking all night."

"You don't act drunk."

"I'm not. It didn't do any good. I just kept getting sober."

"Thank God for that small blessing. What did you want to talk about?"

"Oh, Arthur," she said, tears starting in her eyes, "you've got to help me. I don't know what to do."

"You know I want to help, Vicki. I didn't want all this damned bitterness. But what can I do? Every time we talk, you go off."

"That's what scares me, Arthur. Look at the way I've acted. You know that isn't me. I'm afraid I'm losing my mind."

119

"Sometimes I think so too, but I know you're not. You're just so damned full of hate it's destroying you."

"But what can I do? Every time I think of you and that, that—"

"Watch it."

"Oh, of *her*, I go wild. I go out of my mind, darling, and all I want to do is kill you both. Of course I won't, I love you so and what I really want is to get you back, but I just don't know what I'm doing. The thing is, darling, I've never said this to you before, I know I've been proud and silly but I can't help that now, the thing is I can't do without you, Arthur. I *can't*. You're my life. I've been stupid and belittled you and thought I had to have everything my own way, but darling, I know better than that now. Can't you see I've learned? Won't you give me another chance? I'll do anything, dearest, anything, if you'll just break this off and let us start over like we used to be. I don't even care if you have to spend another night with her to tell her goodbye. I won't even hate her, Arthur, and I'll never say anything against her again. But don't throw us away. The children need you, honey, but it's not for them I'm asking. It's for me, and for you. No matter what I may have said, you're the most wonderful man in the world for me. The only man. And I'm the woman for you. You've taught me my lesson, baby. Can't we, please, be happy now?"

She lifted her tear-stained face to his, her eyes naked with pleading, and he bent to kiss her whiskey mouth. With a sob, she came into his arms like a child, holding him close while her lips circled his.

"Oh, darling," she said at last, "you do love me, don't you? And you'll try again?"

"I've told you, Vicki," he said, pulling her head down on his shoulder, "I hope I always feel love for you, but things are over between us. I love Zelda, and I'm going to marry her."

"You mean you're leaving me?"

"I am."

She shuddered violently, burying her face in his neck. For a long time he held her quietly, stroking her until the shuddering subsided into a steady trembling.

"And what's to become of me?" she said.

120

"That's up to you, Vicki. I don't see why you'll have much trouble. You've always made a fetish of being self-reliant."

"Jesus, Arthur," she said, alive again in her contempt, "are you really stupid? That was just a game I played with myself and everybody else. I've never been self-reliant in my life."

"You sure put on a good act."

"And look what it got me. When are you leaving?"

"Whatever's the right time for all of us."

"Will you wait a little? Give me some time to get used to it and get the children prepared? You can see her too if you like. I won't bother you."

"You know I'll do anything that will help, Vicki."

"And will you do me one more favor? Will you make love to me now?"

In one quick motion she shook off her negligee and sat naked beside him. Her neck was ringed with bruises.

"Jesus," he said, "I really got you, didn't I? I'm sorry, baby. I was kind of out of my mind too."

"It's all right. I had it coming. Please, darling, make love to me now."

"Just for love?"

"Just for love. No obligations."

He bent to kiss her, but she held him back.

"Be my guest," she said, loosened his robe, and gently, almost reverently, began to kiss his body.

121

17

Had he only imagined it, Arthur wondered, the silence that enveloped the writer department when he paused at the door? But he knew he had not. Two girls were in their places at the long benches which lined the room, heads bent over the assemblies on which each performed her own operation before passing them on to the right. Everything looked usual enough—each in her accustomed place, Ulysses erect at the front like a schoolmaster proctoring an examination to which his students were dutifully attentive.

Situation normal. Only the quiet was wrong. Unquestionably, they had been talking about him and Zelda.

"How's it going, Ulysses?" he asked, striding briskly into the room.

"Not so good, Mr. Evans," Uylsses said, turning with a look in which dolefulness struggled unsuccessfully with joy. "We're starting to have trouble."

"What kind of trouble?"

"With the new part."

"Why trouble? Everything's been going fine."

"We're startin on the new batch," Ulysses said patiently, his little eyes bright with hate. "It don't fit right. The ratchet don't engage."

"How do you mean, the ratchet doesn't engage? It's the same part, isn't it?"

"Sposed to be."

"Then why doesn't it work?"

"Dunno," Ulysses said with a shrug. "Ain't figured the trouble yet."

"I must say you sound pretty damned cheerful about it," Arthur said. "Show me what you mean."

"Gimme that last one you finished, Mamie," Ulysses said, going up to a stout middle-aged woman in the front row. "See here? The clearance ain't right. It goes on all right, but the ratchet don't engage when you press the keys."

Probably the one who made the calls, Arthur thought, studying the sullen face bent silently over her assembly while Ulysses demonstrated the problem. There was no doubt about it. The part did not work. Would never work.

"I thought you said you didn't know what was wrong," Arthur said sharply. "The trouble is obvious. They've cut it wrong."

"I mean I don't know how they cut it wrong yet," Ulysses said aggressively. "There's three places it could be off. Here, see, and here, and—"

"When did you start having this trouble?"

"Just this morning. Those five are the first ones Mamie used the new batch on."

"Have you called Watkins yet?"

"Nossir, I tell you we just found it. We was just talking about it. I was gonna measure and then talk to you."

"So that's what you were talking about. All right, let's go back to the bench and check. I'll call Watkins myself."

The chatter began while they walked to the back of the room, the familiar hum with its faint note of mockery, unidentifiable but unmistakable. He felt it like a current while Ulysses measured, squinting over his gauge. Ulysses was all seriousness now, shifting his calipers like a surgeon, checking, rechecking, hemming and hawing until Arthur began to feel like a figure in a Keystone comedy. Any minute now, he thought, comes the pie in the face. He was about to protest when a burst of giggles broke out in Mamie's sector.

"All right now," Ulysses shouted in a voice Arthur had never heard. "How d'ya expect me to figure this out when you're cacklin like a bunch of hens? Shut up and get to work."

While Arthur watched with new respect, he studied the part until at last he glanced up with a puzzled look on his face.

"It don't make sense, Mr. Evans," he said. "It checks out perfect. To the thousandth."

"You mean it's the right size? To tell you the truth, Ulysses, I thought you'd arranged to have it wrong."

"I wouldn't do that, Mr. Evans," Ulysses said indignantly. "I wouldn't put no bad parts in my writers."

"I have some idea of the things you'd do, Ulysses," Arthur said. "The things you have done. But I'll talk to you about that later. You mean that as far as you can tell this part is the right size?"

"Far as I can measure it. Lemme check it against one of my spares."

He dug into a drawer and came up with another piece, which he fitted deftly against the first. The alignment was perfect.

"Damn if I understand it, Mr. Evans," he said. "It oughta work."

The hostility was gone, Arthur noted with a kind of detached interest, and once again they were master and man, united in a common problem. Maybe, he thought, just maybe if I'd understood things before, all this wouldn't have had to happen. But that was ancient history, history like the calls to Vicki. The problem was now, it was blind children like Janie, and blind adults like Vicki and Zelda and himself, lost in a maze to which Ulysses held the key. Unfortunately, the key was to a trap door, triggered somewhere along the path ahead to drop them on their keisters and chute them into a wherewhen in the secret world of never. Loud applause.

"How many spares do you have, Ulysses?" he asked.

"About twenty-five."

"All right. Have Mamie take off the new parts she's put on and use the spares to fix those and as many more as you can. Give me one, along with a new one, and you keep one. We'll figure it out somehow. Meanwhile, keep the subassemblies moving."

Back in his office, he sat fingering the two parts, matching them instinctively and finding no flaw. Vicki smiled at him, from her picture, serene and matronly, bastioned by well-scrubbed children, neat and self-conscious. Automatically, the parts moving in his left hand, he took the picture and thrust it in his bottom drawer, into the miscellany of unfiled reports, used paperclips, and tired rubber bands. Requiescat in pieces.

Unquestionably, Ulysses was on the level. Whatever was wrong, it was not his doing. Luck, that cheerful whore, that rat who deserted lost causes, had made her decision, cast her lot with the enemy, and teamed with malice to assure their downfall. It was an omen, and for the first time since the morning he had declared himself to Zelda, fear gripped him, the doom whose ring he had then thought to escape. How fight an enemy

124

who refused to exist, who struck from within the confines of his own beleagured soul? Whose chief weapon was himself?

"What's the matter, darling?" Zelda said.

He had not even heard her come in.

"God, am I glad to see you," he said. "Come here and kiss me. Maybe you'll help me snap out of it."

"Was she as rough as that?" she said, coming around the desk and laying her cheek against his. "Oh, darling, I thought about you all night. I hardly slept at all."

"Then that makes three of us. Vicki and I were at it practically all night."

"I thought so. How did it go?"

"Awful. Worse than I could tell you. I didn't know Vicki could be like that. I hit her, finally. In fact, I damn near choked her to death."

"Darling," she said, "how awful. Has it made you do that to yourselves? Does it have to be that way, baby? And can you stand it? I don't want to make you violate yourself."

"I can stand it," he said. "I can stand anything. Though God knows it's not easy. I didn't mean it to be this way, Zel. We're all right for a while, almost loving sometimes, and then all of a sudden Vicki's after me and I fight back. It's awful."

"And are you sure it's worth it, Arthur? Are you absolutely damned sure? You've got to be, you know. I couldn't bear your hating us afterwards for something you'd come to feel I made you do."

"You know I'd never do that, Zel. You're worth anything."

"Then you've got to understand me, Arthur," she said, laying her lean hand on his shoulder, "how I feel about all this. How I feel about Vicki. I don't hate her, you know, not the way she does me. I don't have to. Now. But I can, if she threatens me the way I have her. We're enemies, darling, she and I, right down to the final animal inside us. Don't fool yourself it'll ever be friendly. We're both fighting for our man, and we'd kill each other to get him. Your two women are more alike than you realize, lover, only with this difference. I'll fight for you, all out, as long as you know you want us. The minute you don't, I won't raise a hand to keep you. I'll even help you pack."

"Jesus, Zelda," he said, rising to kiss her, "don't suitcase me yet. Not before I move in, anyway."

125

"Not suitcasing you, baby," she said, "not till you ask for it. Just want you to be sure, that's all."

"You know I'm sure. I think even Vicki's beginning to. At least we were rational this morning. I think we began to get somewhere finally."

"I hope so, honey. But it kills me to see you so depressed. It almost broke my heart to see you sitting there like that when I came in. As if you didn't know whether school kept and didn't care."

"I guess I did look pretty miserable. But it wasn't last night I was thinking about. It's something that happened just this morning. We're having trouble with the new part."

"Oh, no. Is it serious?"

"Plenty. The new batch won't work. Period. I thought Ulysses had rigged it, but he's as puzzled as I am."

"You mean that on top of everything else the son of a bitch is getting lucky too?"

"It looks that way," he said with a grin. "It's pretty funny if you want to think about it."

"Then get set for a real belly laugh, lover. Guess who's on the way over?"

"Vicki?"

"Somebody even sweeter. Henry Maynard."

"Henry? What the hell does he want? He never set foot in here in his life except for Board meetings."

"He didn't say. Just said to tell you he'd be here in fifteen minutes. Looks like Vicki's not the only one gets telephone calls."

"You think Ulysses put a burr up Henry's ass too?"

"I know damn well he did. You forget, Arthur, he was desperate. Things were going too well. Until this morning. God, it's a riot."

She laughed, a rich, warm laugh, joyous and free.

"It's not so damned funny as all that," he said, grinning in spite of himself.

"But don't you see, baby," she said, "it is just that funny. I was thinking about Ulysses. All that scheming he did, and scared of it too, because he isn't sure just how people like you and Vicki will react. It might have all blown up in his face, but he had to do it anyway, you see, because it was his last chance. And now that stupid part comes along and does the job for him without his lifting a hand. So now he's back there kicking himself in the ass, hoping he didn't louse up the deal by being too eager. Oh, darling, it's rich."

She laughed again, and he joined her freely, his soul serene.

"God, Zelda," he said, joy alive in him, "you don't know what you do for me. Before you came in I was a miserable bastard, and now look at us. Laughing like a couple of idiots."

"What we do for each other," she said, putting her hands on his shoulders. "Do you think I'd feel like this if I were still alone? Kiss me."

"Just the time for Henry to come in," he said when he released her. "Give him the picture in a way even he can understand."

"Why not clean off the desk and do it right? Hey, you moved the picture."

"Did I? I guess I did. So it's a symbol. Let's get the show on the road now, baby, and get me down there looking respectable for Henry."

"What are you going to tell him?"

"How do I know? It's his show. I can wait. Come on, now. Kiss me and get going. Now that you've revived me, I've got to think."

"Hell of a note," she said. "All these years and I have to pick a bossy bastard like you."

"Just lucky, I guess," he said cheerfully, his hand on the buttock where it was now at home. "Thank God you don't wear a girdle. I love you, Zelda, and don't forget it."

"I don't," she said, stretching up to kiss him. "Never. And don't forget I do you."

He watched her walk to the door with the confident stride that was perhaps the first thing he had loved in her. Now there was Henry Maynard. Am I to understand you are engaged in an illicit affair with Zelda Huckaby, Arthur? I love her, if that's what you mean. Love? Harumph. Immorality is not love, Arthur. But how did this deplorable condition come about? Well, it's like this, Henry baby. I watched her walk, see, and then first thing you know—

Why not? Henry would understand that as little as anything else. Vicki spoke for Henry's mind, for the Henhouse, and for

127

Phoenix as well. Except for Captain Tom. And perhaps Doc Flint.

Not bad odds at that.

Back at the desk, the gap where the picture had been stared at him. Where had he put the damned thing? Something about it gnawed at him, but he couldn't remember touching it at all. He'd come back from talking to Ulysses and sat there thinking about of course. The bottom drawer. His own private mare's nest. Trust the old subconscious to be on the ball.

But there was something else. Something that went along with the picture. Something in his left hand.

The parts. He'd been playing with them while he unconsciously disposed of the picture, feeling their improbable symmetry, feeling.

Hey!

He picked them up in his left hand again, slipping them together until they matched. There was no doubt of it. The difference was plain. But was it important? He racked his uncertain memories of the Taliaferro's insides, seeking a justification for his certainty about the plan now forming in his mind. There had to be something. Damn it, he *knew*.

Captain Tom. Tolerance. His concise explanation, luminous with drunkenness, of the virtues of Ulysses' engineering. It had to be the answer. And it was exactly the kind of thing that Ulysses, vainly scenting the false hare of measurement, would overlook until he had exhausted every possibility to which he could apply his gauges. Time enough for Arthur to show him a thing or two, and to throw old Henry off stride.

He was going through the mail when the buzzer announced Henry's arrival.

"Send him in," he said into the intercom. "And stand by, will you, Zel? I'm going to want you in a few minutes."

Had he ever really seen Henry Maynard before, he wondered as Zelda ushered him in. The undistinguished figure was immaculate in another of the endless succession of new suits in which he sought to adorn himself. An ordinary body swathed in expensive cloth, topped by a balding head and meaningless face to which the trim moustache brought no precision. Eyes soft and restless, at once frightened and furtive. Thin lips parted

128

in the tentative smile which preceded the grim line that signified disapproval.

By God, he thought, he's just as frightened as Zelda says. The anemic little peasant. He grinned.

"Well, Henry," he said, rising and extending his hand. "This is a welcome surprise. We don't often have this pleasure."

Maynard's hand was as limp as his cuffs were crisp.

"Just thought I'd stop by," he said, nervously precise. "It's getting close to time for our special meeting, and I thought, as Chairman of the Board, that I'd better see how things are going. Everything's fine, I hope."

He hitched his pants up carefully, pinching them neatly at the crease the same distance about each knee, sat down, and crossed one trim ankle over the other.

"Been following my weekly reports, I suppose?" Arthur said, slouching back in his chair and beginning to fill a pipe.

"Indeed yes. Most encouraging too."

"But you just thought something might have gone wrong today?"

Henry's smile wavered.

"I do have responsibilities, you know, Arthur," he said sharply, "responsibilities which I do not take lightly. To the best of my ability, I attempt to carry them out."

"You misunderstood me, Henry," Arthur said gently. "I wasn't being critical. On the contrary, I was impressed by your perception. We do have a problem, one which just developed this morning. In fact, in view of its urgency, I was about to call you to ask if you could come over to discuss it with us. But you anticipated me, I'm pleased to say."

"Well, of course," Maynard said, settling back slightly in the straight chair, "if I can be of any use, I'll be glad, Arthur. Though if it's a technical matter, I don't know how valuable my opinion will be."

"It's technical, all right," Arthur said, reaching for the intercom, "though I suspect what's needed to solve it is only a little common sense, a quality that sometimes seems in short supply around here. Let me get Ulysses. It's his department."

Did he only imagine the flicker of uncertainty in Henry's eyes? Probably yes. Let's not go overboard just because you've been seeing his essence, he counseled himself. He's been at this game a long time, you know, and he's not as simple as he seems right now.

Zelda dispatched, he smiled at Henry and made an elaborate business of lighting his pipe.

"I hope this won't take too long, Arthur," Henry said. "There are some other items I thought we ought to get straightened out in advance of the meeting."

"If we don't get this one straightened out," Arthur said grimly, "we may have an entirely different kind of meeting. But it shouldn't take long. Zelda will be back with Ulysses in a minute."

The flicker again?

"Mighty efficient girl, Zelda," he volunteered. "Don't know what I'd do without her."

"Indeed," said Henry Maynard. "Her father was a fine man."

"For a Cracker."

"For a Cracker," Henry agreed gravely. "Although it's one of my basic principles, Arthur, that what counts is what a man *is,* not where he came from. If more of our young people understood this today—"

He broke off as Zelda came in with Ulysses, rising politely, his trousers straightening in an unbroken line precisely to his shoe tops.

There was no doubt about Ulysses' agitation. His florid face was stained a deeper hue, and his bright eyes shifted nervously, looking anywhere except at Arthur and Henry.

"Have a seat, Ulysses," Arthur said, keeping his seat and signaling Zelda to the chair beside the desk. "You remember Mr. Maynard, the Chairman of our Board?"

"Yessir," Ulysses said, edging onto the front of a chair. "I know Mr. Maynard."

"Fine. Then why don't you explain to him the nature of the difficulty we've encountered with the new part?"

"Can't explain it," Ulysses said sullenly. "Ain't figured it out yet."

"I didn't ask you for the solution, Ulysses. Just tell him what the problem is."

"Just tell me in your own words, Ulysses," Henry Maynard said helpfully. "What seems to be the difficulty?"

"Well," Ulysses said, "there's this new part, see, the one we're usin in this modification Mr. Evans wanted and all of a sudden the new batch we started puttin on this morning don't work, that's all."

"And you weren't having any trouble before?" Henry Maynard asked.

"Didn't say we didn't have no trouble," Ulysses said. "Had to change the whole production line around. But the part was working till now."

"You had to change one operation," Arthur said sharply. "Mamie's. And it took her two weeks to get the idea when she should have learned it in an hour. But never mind that. Tell Mr. Maynard what happened this morning."

"It's kind of hard to explain when you can't see it."

"Here, use these for illustration. Catch."

Abruptly, the two parts were in the air, falling in a gentle arc toward Ulysses, who managed to snare one and lurch after the other. Sprawled awkardly to retrieve it, one hand on the floor, one grasping the chair leg, he gave Arthur a look of pure hatred.

"Sorry, Ulysses," he said calmly. "I guess I'm not the pitcher I used to be. Straighten up now and show Mr. Maynard what the trouble is. Explain the difference in the parts to him."

"But damn it, Mr. Evans," Ulysses said, coming slowly erect, red-faced and furious, "excuse me, Miss Huckaby, but there ain't no difference. That's the trouble."

"But I don't understand," Henry Maynard said. "If they're the same, what's the problem?"

"I don't *know* what the trouble is," Ulysses said, tears forming in the corners of his eyes. "They ought to work but they don't. The ratchet don't engage. The piece fits but the goddamn keys don't go down. I don't know what the hell's wrong. Everything was all right until we started messin around with this damn modification. Now it's all gone to hell. And it ain't my fault."

Sobs racked him as he glared at them, and he buried his face in his hands.

"It's all right, Ulysses," Arthur said gently. "It's not your fault. None of it. Not even the phone calls. You couldn't help those any more than you could help breaking down now. That's why you need somebody to look after you. That's why you've got to let me make the decisions and not try to interfere. I won't let you down, Ulysses. But you've got to play it straight with

131

me too. Now sit up like man and I'll show you what the trouble is."

"The trouble?" Ulysses said, lifting his great head. "You mean you know what it is?"

"Of course I do. Match the two parts up and hold them out to me."

"Like this?"

"That's right. Now which is the new one?"

"I can't tell you, Mr. Evans. You know that."

"It's the one you caught."

"I done forgot, Mr. Evans. I got too upset."

"Then we'll do it another way. How are you holding those, Ulysses?"

"The way they match, Mr. Evans," Ulysses said, looking at the fat thumb and forefinger between which the parts nestled. "The way you told me."

"I didn't tell you *how* to hold them, Ulysses. You did that automatically. What we're looking for is the way they don't match, right?"

"Yessir."

"Then take one in each hand and rub them between your fingers."

"Yessir."

"Feel any difference?"

"Well, by God," Ulysses said, a smile lighting his face, "beggin your pardon, Miss Zelda, but he's got it. Now why the hell didn't I figure that out?"

"Would somebody please tell me what's going on?" Henry Maynard said. "I must say it's the most curious performance I ever saw in a place of business. I'm surprised at you both."

"Tell him, Ulysses," Arthur said.

"It's simple, Mr. Maynard," Ulysses said. "The new part's too rough. They forgot to buff it, probably. With the fine tolerance we got on that machine, it jams before the ratchet can engage. I can have these things smoothed down in no time. We won't lose no time at all."

"Then get with it, Ulysses," Arthur said. "Now you're on the ball."

"Right away, sir. But I'd like to say somthin first."

"Shoot."

"It's about them calls, Mr. Arthur. I wanta apologize."

"Do we have to waste time on this?" Henry Maynard said. "I've already told you I have other things to talk about, Arthur, and I don't have all morning. That will do now, Ulysses. And thank you for your trouble."

"You just hold it, Henry," Arthur said. "We have plenty of time for this, and you're going to listen. Go ahead, Ulysses."

"I just wanta say I'm sorry, Mr. Arthur. You're a good man, and I should of trusted you. I will from now on. I fixed them calls to your wife, and I wish I hadn't. I called Mr. Maynard too, and I talked to him before, but I reckon you know about that anyhow. I got nothin against you and Miss Zelda. You're good people, both of you, the best we ever had around here, and I'm sure sorry for anything I did to make trouble for you. I know you didn't like me to mention talkin to you, Mr. Maynard," he said, turning to Henry, "but Mr. Arthur's smart enough he knows about it already. He's the boss, Mr. Maynard, and I ain't goin to lie to him no more. Now, if you don't mind, I'll get on with those parts."

"Do that, Ulysses," Arthur said. "And I want you to know I appreciate what you've said. Will you do one thing for me?"

"Anything you say, Mr. Arthur."

"Give Watkins hell, will you? For both of us. Only maybe you ought to thank them too."

"Yessir. But I'll keep the thanks to myself."

"You're a big, beautiful bear, Ulysses," Zelda said as he shambled toward the door. "I'd kiss you if I didn't have to sit here and take notes."

"Some other time, Miss Zelda," he said without breaking stride. "Only don't make my girls jealous. I got obligations, you know."

"Notes?" Henry Maynard said as the door closed behind Ulysses. "Do you mean you're making a record of this, Zelda? That's an invasion of privacy."

"Not just *a* record, Henry," Arthur said. "A complete stenographic record. Every word. Among other things, Zelda is an excellent secretary."

"Katherine Gibbs, forty-two," Zelda said. "I don't miss a word, Henry."

"What's the point of a trick like this?"

"It's no trick, Henry," Arthur said. "Just a precaution, in case you're planning the kind of trouble I think you are. Something to read at the next Board meeting."

"It would just be your word against mine."

"Not quite, Henry. Ulysses will swear to everything he heard, and I don't think the Board will have much trouble believing the rest of it."

"Now wait a minute, Arthur," Henry said, the grim line tilting into a smile that was almost pleading. "Let's not be unreasonable. I'll admit I had some things wrong when I came here today. Ulysses, for one. I guess I overestimated him."

"And underestimated me."

"That too, perhaps. I know you don't like it that he talked to me, but what else could I do, Arthur? He wanted to, and as President of the Board I had an obligation to listen. You understand that, don't you?"

"You could have told me about it."

"I should have, Arthur. I won't make that mistake again. But there are some things I have to talk to you about, and it would be much easier if Miss Huckaby would step outside."

"Zelda stays, Henry. And not just for the record. Don't you think we know what you want to talk about? My God, Ulysses had one of his girls call up Vicki and make all sorts of accusations about us. Say what you want to, and get it off your chest."

"Very well," Henry said, hitching up his trousers and moving forward in his chair. "If you insist. You understand there's nothing personal in this, Zelda, I'm only doing my duty."

"I know," she said. "Just call me Tiny Tim. Get on with it, Henry."

"All right. Ulysses made some very serious accusations. He acused you of having an illicit affair and said it was the talk of the Institute."

"Ulysses wouldn't say that now."

"You're quite right, I'm sure. You beat him down rather thoroughly. But the fact remains that he did say it, and that he made a very convincing case. In my capacity as Chairman of the Board, I am asking you now, reluctant as I am to do so, whether this accusation is true. Nothing would make me happier than for you to say it is not. I need no further assurance."

134

"It's none of your business, Henry," Arthur said after a slight pause.

"It's *what*?"

"I said it's none of your goddamn business. My private life is my own affair. So is Zelda's. The fact that we both happen to work here has nothing to do with it."

"Now wait a minute, Arthur. You misunderstand me entirely. I certainly have no desire to probe into your personal life. But an illicit affair here within the confines of the Taliaferro Institute is no longer personal business. The reputation of the Institute is our mutual responsibility, Arthur, and I am sure you would be the first to agree that we cannot permit the slightest breath of scandal to sully it."

"Sully it, my ass," Arthur said, leaning forward in his chair. "This goddam Institute was founded in scandal. If the old Judge hadn't been drunk and made his wife drive that horse that blinded her, there never would have been one in the first place. I'm tempted just to say *bullshit*, Henry, but I'll tell you a story instead."

"That would certainly be preferable to the language you've just been employing," Henry said, his mouth the grim line. "I trust you're making a record of this, Zelda?"

"Every syllable," she said. "One *l* in bullshit, Arthur?"

"Two. Here's the story, Henry. It's about a brilliant old legal counselor for the Pennsylvania Railroad who had a weakness for young girls. He wasn't especially careful about covering it up, and finally one particular bit of gossip got to be too much for the Board of Directors. The Chairman of the Board called him in. He told the old gentleman about it, and informed him that for the sake of the good name of the Pennsylvania Railroad, this sort of thing would have to stop. The old lawyer just looked at him. 'Mr. Chairman,, he said, standing up, *'I've just one thing to say. You can buy my brains, but you can't buy my balls.'* "

"And so,"

"He kept his job. Think about it, Henry. Maybe the message will seep through."

Henry Maynard reddened.

"I would advise you, Arthur," he said, "that insolence is hardly the ideal response to charges as grave as these."

"Insolence, You're the one who's insolent. Asking us impertinent questions and calling it duty. There's one question you have a right to ask, Henry. Are Zelda and I valuable employees of the Institute? If you'd ever taken the trouble to be a Chairman in more than name, you'd have the answer already, but regardless, you got it this morning with Ulysses. We're not just valuable, we're essential. The Institute would be in a hell of a mess without us. Anything else is none of your goddam business, or the Board's, or anybody's else's. Is that clear?"

"Yes, you old goat," Zelda said, "suppose I started to ask you personal questions? You think I don't know about the time you got that Snider woman knocked up and had to pay through the nose to send her off to California? The only reason your wife didn't divorce you then was she liked being Mrs. Maynard and was willing to put up with a jerk like you for the privilege, especially after she had the goods on you. Mae Snider made an affidavit about it for Dad before she left. You didn't know that, did you? I could put my hands on it right now if I looked."

"That is quite enough," Henry Maynard said, his face livid. "Miss Huckaby, you are not a fit employee of the Taliaferro Institute for the Blind, and I shall see to it that you do not remain one. Arthur, you have my sympathy. I'm afraid blood tells after all. I have heard enough to make it perfectly clear how things stand. I am calling a special meeting of the Board of Directors for ten o'clock tomorrow morning, and I am instructing you to see that the proper arrangements are made. I trust that is entirely clear. Good day."

"Well, darling," she said after the door slammed behind Henry's trim ass, "the fat's in the fire now. I shouldn't have made that crack about Mae Snider, but when he called you insolent it just came out. I'm afraid your woman wasn't much help this morning."

"You were marvelous. Do you really have an affidavit?"

"Not any more. Dad burned them before he died, so I wouldn't use them, I guess. He knew my temper better than you do. But he let me read them all first. The story's true."

"Obviously. Don't think I'm sorry. We've got it down to where we want it now, an issue I'm willing to fight on. If they want to fire us for this, I'm ready to go. Especially now that we've made peace with Ulysses. How'd you think that went?"

"Wonderful, darling. You've made Ulysses a friend for life.

136

Whatever happens, the Ohio modification is here to stay. You were marvelous, baby. They didn't even know what hit them. You were like a lion in a den of Christians."

"Then come here, lioness," he said, reaching for her. "Those Christians are scrawny, and I need my meat."

18

A different Vicki awaited him. Icy, swathed in a high-necked blouse, hair impeccable and pinless, she sat in a chair in the livingroom, a drink on the table beside her.

"Jesus, Vicki," he said as he came in, "still at it? The sauce is going to catch up with you if you don't lay off."

"I don't see how that kind of bad joke helps things," she said distinctly, "especially from a man as devoted to the bottle as you are. Now that you've had your dirty crack, why don't you fix your drink? I know how much you want it."

"I could use one, all right," he said, putting his jacket on the back of a chair and heading for the kitchen. "It's been quite a day."

"Yes," she said. "So I heard."

"You what?" he said, stopping short. "Who've you been talking to?"

"Henry Maynard told me."

"Henry? You mean you've been talking to him?"

"I have. I called him about certain matters of mutual concern and was delighted to find that he was an anxious as I to institute preventive measures."

"Are you crazy, Vicki?" he said, advancing a step toward her. "Are you really out of your mind? What possible good do you think you can do by involving Henry?"

"No, I'm not carzy, Arthur. I was never more sane. But before we're through, for your sake, for all our sakes, I hope to convince you how crazy you are. As for involving Henry, I didn't do it. You did, with your antics at the Henhouse. And don't you touch me, Arthur Evans," she said as he came toward her. "I'll call the police if you lay a hand on me. One look at my neck and you'll be in jail. And will you please take your coat off that chair? You know how often I've asked you not to leave it there."

Automatically, out of the habit of years, he turned toward the chair, taking the first step before he caught himself.

"Will you kindly go straight to hell," he said, wheeling back toward the kitchen. "And while I'm waiting, I'll have that drink."

"You might offer to freshen mine," she said. "At least you used to have manners, before you started hanging around with that bitch."

"I've changed," he said over his shoulder. "Since last night I'm taking lessons from my wife."

In the haven of the kitchen he salvaged three ice cubes from the watery mess in the bowl, filled the glass with straight whiskey, and downed half of it in a gulp. The warm liquor sobered him and he looked around the kitchen, the usual mess on Katy's afternoon off. Relaxing in the death of his anger, he fished the last cube from the bowl, poured out the water, and refilled it from the freezer. All right, Arthur, he told himself as he placed the bowl and bottle on a tray, let's knock it off. If you're going to blow up every time she provokes you, what can you expect from her? Somebody's got to stay sane around here.

"Let me have your glass, Vicki," he said with a smile as he put the tray down on the coffee table. "I'm sorry I barked at you. I don't want to fight."

"Here," she said, pushing it at him in a gesture that managed to be contemptuous. "We're not going to fight. You'd better not try. But I do have a few things to say, junior, and you're going to listen."

"Junior? What prompted that?"

"If you act like a child, you can expect to be addressed as one."

"Oh. Okay, Mom. Say on. Here."

"How true that is," she said, accepting her drink. "Only I'm not your mother, Arthur, and it's painful to have to act like it. Don't you think it's pretty depressing, when a grown man forces his wife to act like his mother?"

"I could cheerfully be spared it. But why don't you go on and say what you want to, Vicki? Where are the kids, by the way?"

"I arranged for all of them to spend the night out. I'd rather not have them around to see their father try to choke their mother and the police take him away."

"For Christ's sake, Vicki, I'm not going to choke you. You know that."

"You don't have to swear, Arthur. Do you deny you choked

139

me last night? Do you deny you tried to kill me until I stopped you? Do I have to show you the bruises again? Do you realize I couldn't go out of this house today? That I won't be able to go out for weeks without showing the whole world that my own husband tried to murder me?"

"You said this morning you deserved it."

"I said a lot of foolish things this morning. What do you expect? I was scared to death. But I've had a whole day to think about it, and I'm not scared now. Now sit down and listen, Junior. And take it easy with that drink until I'm finished. I'd like to get some things said while you're still sober enough to understand them."

"For a girl who doesn't want to fight, he said, sitting down in the chair opposite her, "you manage to be plenty aggressive."

"If you can't stand hearing the truth, I can't help it. Now listen, Junior. Have you given any thought whatever to what these ridiculous antics will do to your children? Have already done?"

"Of course I have, Vicki. You must know how I worry about it."

"But the little man has to have his way just the same? The children can lump it as long as he gets his two-bit whore. Did you happen to notice them at breakfast this morning, or were you too anxious to see her to pay attention?"

"I thought breakfast was one of our more pleasant meals. You and I were friendly and the kids were quieter than usual."

"Quiet? You fool, don't you know they were terrified? Waking in the night to hear their father screaming at their mother and choking her? What do you expect? They were afraid you'd strangle them."

"Don't be a bigger jackass than you have to be, Vicki. You were doing most of the screaming. And how do you know they waked up? Did they tell you?"

"Calling me names isn't going to help you any, Arthur. They didn't have to tell me. I could see it on their faces. Did you by any chance happen to notice your daughter Margie?"

"She was quiet, Ill admit that. Has been the past few days. Its impossible not to notice it, though I must say its kind of a pleasant relief."

"Arthur, you're so selfish it's disgusting. The poor child is

140

frightened silly at what you're going to do. If you could think of something besides yourself for once, you'd know what something like this means to a girl her age. Is it really worth it, Arthur, the hurt to that poor, innocent child, just to get your own selfish way?"

"And what do you think you're trying to get?"

"I'm a mother, Arthur, trying to protect my children and my husband who's acting like a child himself. That's what I'm trying to do. Save my home, in spite of your determination to wreck it."

"And is all your hate the way to do it? And all the years of shutting yourself off, of not giving a damn what went on inside me as long as I was a dutiful husband?"

"I don't hate you, Arthur," she said, emptying her glass and holding it out. "Refill, please. I love you, if you only had the brains to understand it. As for shutting myself off, that's just your own sick mind. I've been everything a good wife could be, everything. I said *refill*."

"It's your funeral," he said, taking her glass. "How much have you had already, Vicki? Have you been drinking all day?"

"None of your business. Whatever I've been doing, I've been acting like a responsible wife and mother, looking after my children instead of being out disgracing you before the whole town with some cheap whore."

"For Christ's sake, Vicki," he said, handing her the glass, "put on another record, will you? As for the children, yes, I worry about them. I love them, in my way, despite the fact that I don't seem very close to them any more. But there's nothing I can do. I only existed with you for years. Now that I'm alive, with Zelda, I can't settle for this any more. I literally can't. Jesus, woman, do you call this living? The way we are now? Do you?"

"And do you call it living, Junior, when you're chasing around like a sixteen year old with that cheap little bitch?"

"It's living, Vicki, believe me. But I'll tell you something else. After last night I wouldn't live with you even if Zelda had never been invented. I've had it with you, baby. Up to here."

"Not the way you're going to, sweetie, before you're through. You think you're going to live with her?"

"I plan to."

141

"Then let me tell you something about that. You're on trial at the Henhouse tomorrow, you know. On trial for your life. You understand that?"

"There's a Board meeting, yes. And your friend Henry will try to crucify me."

"Try?" she said with a harsh laugh. "Try? My God, Junior, are you so simple-minded you think he'll have to try? They'll have that bitch out of there and you nailed to the cross so fast it'll make your head swim. Your only chance is to grovel, sonny, tell them how sorry you are and promise to be a good boy and start acting like a respectable husband and father. Then maybe they'll let you off the hook. Maybe. Those are respectable citizens, Junior, grown men, and they don't like your antics any more than I do. The job they'll do on you, buster, by the time they finish your name'll be mud all over the country. They'll run you out of town if you try to go anywhere with that thing. Arthur, when are you going to wise up?"

"All right, Vicki," he said, standing up. "I've heard enough. If you don't have anything more to say, just shut up, will you? Did Katy leave us anything for dinner or do you want to go out?"

"Don't tell me to shut up, Junior. It's *my* house, and I'll talk when I want to. Of course I'm not going out. In this blouse in this weather? I might as well go naked and show people how my husband tried to murder me. But don't think I'm going to fix dinner. Heat it up yourself. I'm through being a slave. Fix me another drink."

"Now listen here, you silly bitch," he said, moving toward her. "I've listened to all the hate from you I'm going to. Either you shut up or I'll —"

"Don't you touch me," she screamed, her eyes wide with fear. "Don't you try to kill me, you bastard. I'll call the police. Right now. They'll fix you, you murderer."

Only when she stood up did he realize how drunk she was. She staggered as soon as she was on her feet, and when she turned to run she began to fall, coming down headlong in mid-stride, face flat on the carpet, arms outstretched and limp.

"Vicki," he said, bending over her, "did you hurt yourself, honey? Are you all right?"

A gentle snore answered him. Her whole body was slack when he rolled her over, her head lolling to one side like a

142

broken flower. He slapped her cheeks sharply, but her only response was a snore.

"You poor fool," he said, stroking the damp curls he had once loved. "Do you have to do this to yourself?"

Gently, his arms under her knees and shoulders, he lifted her and started toward the stairs. She was astonishingly heavy. Her head dangled lifelessly, and before he had taken two steps she jack-knifed so sharply that he barely made it to a chair before she slipped through his arms. She slumped in the cushions, snoring rhythmically.

"The hell with this," he said. "Come on, baby, we'll do it boy scout style."

In an easy motion he had almost forgotten, he looped her arms down his back, bent his shoulder into her middle, and lifted her up. Floated thus like a bag of meal, she rode lightly up the stairs and fell gently on the bed, disheveled and beautiful. And utterly still, only the breathing which fleshed her snores lifting her lovely breasts under the high-necked blouse, ruffling the spittle which formed in the corner of her half-opened mouth.

"Okay, baby," Arthur said, bending to take off her shoes. "Sleep it off. And for God's sake, honey, wake up sane."

Back in the kitchen, he checked the oven to see what Katy had left them. A huge casserole of stew, thick and fragrant. He stuck his finger in the gravy and sucked it thoughtfully. Lamb. His favorite. Good old girl. How long had she been worrying about his stomach? The kitchen in the old house came back to him, striding into its ample darkness after a late tennis match to find his dinner in the warmer on top of the huge coal stove, Katy sitting patiently on her stool by the sink, puffing a corncob pipe, waiting to make sure it suited him before trudging home with her papersack of leftovers. When the world was beautiful and new, and nights like this one could never be.

Shit. Even thought he knew it would hurt her, even at the price of the useless explanation to which she would listen disbelievingly, knowing only that somehow she had displeased him, he couldn't eat that stew. Not tonight. I'm sorry, old girl, he thought while he put the casserole in the refrigerator; finding some cold fried chicken which he carried into the living room. I can't go it tonight. I'll make it up to you somehow.

So. Here they were again. Only more so. And a lovely little meeting coming up tomorrow at which Henry's malice would now parade in the impregnable righteousness of a wronged wife's pleas. Immortality rampant! Turpitude unbounded! He could see it all, and suddenly he knew that it was no longer fun, that for all their love they would not emerge unscathed, that the slime would cling and part of them would accept it as their due.

He had to get out. The house oppressed him, the memory of Vicki drugged on their bed, slobbering and bereaved. He had to talk. But not to Zlda. Not now. Not yet. He looked at his watch. If he hurried, Tom would still be on his plateau. He had to be. God help Arthur Evans if he weren't. Desperately, he hurried to the phone.

19

"You mean," Captain Tom said, "Henry really means to have a witch hunt over you and Zelda tomorrow?"

"He sure as hell does," Arthur said, "and with Vicki's gallant assistance."

"After Mae Snider?"

"You know about that?"

"Of course I know about it. And so does most of the Board. Which is why you can't make any defense on that ground."

"You confuse me, Tom," Arthur said, reaching for the bottle. "Jesus, man, I came here hoping you'd straighten me out. I've had enough confusion the last twenty-four hours to do me the rest of my life."

"The beginning of wisdom," the Captain said. "You can fill mine too. I suppose Zelda had some hopes that might stop Henry."

"She gave it to him straight, all right. I don't think she even thought about what it might do. All it accomplished was to make Henry mad enough to call a meeting."

"Makes no matter. It was only a question of time. Once Henry was on the scent, there was no chance he'd let it alone. So you converted Ulysses?"

"I think so. It's the one thing the last few days that's worked. He's a pretty good man underneath, you know."

"Sure he is. When he's on your side. I'm glad you won that one, Arthur. *Sub speciae aeternitas,* or something about like that, it's the important issue. But it's not the question now."

"Amen," Arthur said. "Ask Vicki. Ask the whole goddamn town when she and Henry get finished."

"Vicki," the Captain said musingly. "I wish I'd seen her."

"So do I," Arthur said. "In my place. I must say, old friend, you've got queer tastes."

"May be, Arthur. But maybe not. You get queer ideas, you know, sitting there in this wheelchair. But you get some right ones, too. About the importance of being alive, for one thing."

"And you think that's living, to quote myself to Vicki, what she and I've been doing? Jesus, man, I wish you the joy of it."

"Which I just might take," the Captain said, "if I were able to get up and do it. It's better than giving up like Margaret did. I'm not the only corpse in this house, you know, Arthur. Not even the first one."

"I'm sorry, Tom," Arthur said. "I'm so wound up in myself I just didn't think. I'm truly sorry."

In the ravaged figure in the wheelchair, the handsome, dissipated face still proud above the wasted body, he saw the man the Captain once had been, elegant, erect, and undefeated, and in the compassion of this vision he was suddenly freed from his own trauma, liberated once again to view them all with the objectivity that was his salvation and his doom.

"Sorry for what?" Captain Tom said. "That I got my ass shot up for messing around with things I could have been smart enough to leave alone? I'm past regretting that, Arthur. It happened, that's all, and I've lived with it so long it's hard to remember anything else. That Margaret turned out to be a limp rag, a pretty face with a jelly soul? I do regret that one, because I knew better. I'm not sorry I went to that strike meeting, because it was the right thing to do, but I wish I'd been bright enough to kick Margaret in the ass and marry Maud."

"Maud Pickett, you mean?" Arthur said, drunk on objectivity. "That old battleaxe?"

"Now there, my boy," the Captain said, holding out his glass for a refill, "you show yourself for the young whippersnapper you are. She was certainly an elderly party to you, in fact she'd be seventy-five this month if she were alive today and that's some years older than I am, but I loved her just the same, even if I was too stupid to admit it."

"I didn't realize, Tom," Arthur said. "I shouldn't have said that either."

"Of course you should, damn it," the Captain said, accepting a new drink. "Are you going to spend the whole goddam night apologizing? I'm glad you're loose enough to be honest. But that doesn't make you right. What do you think you love Zelda for? Her cute little ass?"

"You've got to admit it's nice."

"Of course it is. But so is Vicki's. Nicer. She's a good looking

146

woman, Arthur, even though you may be tired of her. Probably a better fuck too, if you don't mind my saying so."

"Suppose I do mind?"

"Then I'll say it anyway," Tom said, grinning at him. "You called my love a battleaxe. Christ, man, don't you even know what you love Zelda for? Maybe you'd better go back to Vicki."

"All right, Tom," Arthur said, "you got me. I don't know how you know it, but you're right. Vicki and I were better at first. In bed I mean. But not now. Not after Zelda and I had the time to make it different."

"And why is it different?"

"Because it's for a different reason, damn it. For something inside."

"Like a cunt?"

"No, goddamn it. Don't be funny. It's communion, Tom. A meeting of the deepest part of us. Our souls."

"Souls, by God," the Captain said, raising his glass. "I toast you, you young idiot. If I could get out of this goddamn chair, I'd do a dance. You've got it, boy, the thing these righteous bastards like Henry Maynard yap about and never understand. The world of the spirit, Arthur, the kingdom that's within you. Fucking your way to eternity. I had it once, you know, with a girl I knew in France, and then came back after the war like a damned fool and married a jellyfish. If you've got it with Zelda, boy, hold on to it. Fight for it. If you give it up, you deserve to, and I wish you and Vicki well."

"I'm holding all right, Tom. Or will if I survive. Of if Zelda doesn't say the hell with it after all the misery she's going to get."

"Now there's a stupid remark," the Captain said, "if ever I heard one. She won't give up, buddy. It's you I'm worried about."

"But that session's not going to be easy for her tomorrow, Tom. Henry'll make it rough on her after she let him have it over Mae Snider. You know that."

"Damn right I know it. And what do you plan to do about it?"

"I wish I knew. Fight the best way I can, I guess. Tell them it's none of their damned business and try to make it stick."

"Fat chance you'll have unless you get somebody going for you. Henry'll take them all with him unless there's somebody

147

out there running interference for you. Who's it going to be?"

"Doc, I guess. He's our only hope."

"Doc can't do this one for you. Not when Henry puts on the robes of righteousness. Doc's reputation is against you, Arthur. You know that. He's never given enough of a damn to be discreet, and he's in no position to say that scandal doesn't matter. It matters to Henry, and to Floyd Butler, and to Frank Newton and all the rest of them. They're all secretly envious of Doc, but they can't afford to approve of him. Christ, boy, half the women in this town, including some of their wives, are afraid to be alone in his office with him."

"And the other half can't wait."

"That's right. But that's no help to you. So who's it going to be?"

"God knows. I guess I have to do it myself."

"Arthur," the Captain said, taking a long swig and holding his glasses up to squint through it, "I swear Vicki's addled your brains. Beautiful sight, isn't it? Consoling. Use your head, man, use it for something besides worrying. Who's the obvious choice?"

"There isn't any, damn it, and you know it. That's why I'm about to drown myself in that beautiful sight of yours. We're stuck."

"How about me?"

"*You*?"

"Yes, me. Thomas Carter III. Remember?"

"But Tom, you left the Board before I came to the Henhouse. You haven't been to a meeting since your accident."

"Like hell I left it. I was appointed for life, and nobody's ever removed me. I'm as legal as the rest of them."

"But that's only a formality, Tom. Sort of a recognition of the Carter family. You haven't really been a member. Henry won't stand for it."

"He'll stand for what I tell him to stand for, Arthur. As for really being a member, I know more about the Henhouse and the work there than the rest of them put together. Sure, they go to meetings, but that's all they do. You leave Henry to me, boy. The main thing is, will you accept my services?"

"*Accept*?" Arthur said, rising and beginning to stride around Tom's plateau as if it were his office at the Henhouse. For the first time he really saw the room, letting it absorb him while

148

his mind played with a whole new set of possibilities, seeing how comfortable S. T.'s ingenuity had made it, a tight little universe where everything, books, papers, bottles, glasses, tobacco, the breathing litter of Captain Tom's remaining pleasures, was scattered in easy reach of that dead body's hand.

"So you're a pacer," the Captain said, rolling himself over to get a fresh bottle. "I was too, once. Do you accept?"

"Accept?" Arthur said, coming over to lay his hand on Tom's bony shoulder. "Man, I could kiss you. You've thought of the one thing that'll throw Henry off stride."

"Suppose you leave that part of the work to Zelda," Tom said, handing him the bottle, "and make yourself useful with this. We'll throw him off stride all right. We'll throw him right out of the Chairmanship. You want to go that far?"

"Damn right I do. It'll be either Henry or me. It has to be. We can never work together after this."

"Then so be it. I can't guarantee miracles, Arthur, but I've got a hunch we can swing it. He won't be figuring on this, and Henry's gift is not for adapting to the unexpected. Now let's drink to it, and then for once I'm going to sleep less than blotto. Your health."

As they were toasting, the phone on the chair rang.

"Why yes, Vicki," the Captain said. "He's right here. You want to talk to him?"

"Hi, honey," Arthur said, taking the receiver, "I guess you got my note. How do you feel?"

"Frightful," Vicki said, turning an adjective into an accusation. "How did you expect? Did you carry me upstairs? I don't remember going."

"I did. You passed out on the rug."

"Well, thank you for that, at least. I gather you didn't choke me again. I couldn't find any new bruises."

"Let's not start that again, Vicki," Arthur said, gesturing helplessly to the Captain. "Is there something you want me to do?"

"Yes, there is, Arthur," she said, her voice sober and cold. "That's why I called, I can't stand this any longer. I don't like myself the way I was tonight. Or last night. We've got to reach a decision. I want to ask you a question, Arthur, and I want you to give me a straight answer. No games or doubletalk, just the

149

simple truth, hard as it may be for you. The children and I have had all we can take of your antics, Arthur, and you've got to choose. Now. It's either your family or Zelda Huckaby, and you can't evade the decision any longer. I know how much you'd like to have your cake and eat it too, but I'm tired of humoring this particular kind of insanity. So which is it going to be, Arthur? You have to decide."

"You mean now you're telling *me* I have to give up Zelda or we're through?"

"I suppose to your twisted mind that seems the logical way to put it. A normal person would say it's time you quit your junior grade antics and took up your responsibilities to your family. But you get the idea."

"Vicki," he said, taking the drink the Captain handed him, "if I had your passion for name-calling, I'd tell you you were nuts. Don't you remember how many times I told you, last night and then again tonight, that we were through regardless? So I'll tell you again. We're finished, Vicki, finished. I won't give up Zelda. I'm going to marry her. But even if she drops dead in the next ten minutes, even if I never see her again in my life, you and I have had it. And for good. Is that clear?"

He finished his drink with the phone silent against his ear, and passed it to the Captain for refill.

"Did you hear me, Vicki?" he said at last. "Are you still there?"

"I'm here, Arthur," she said quietly, "and I heard you, loud and clear. All right, if that's how it is, so be it. I hate it, but it's better than the way we've been. I'd appreciate it if you didn't come home, Arthur. Right now it would only upset me, and I'd like a good night's sleep before I face the children in the morning. I'll send your clothes to the office tomorrow."

"All right, Vicki," he said, elation and loss overwhelming him. "I'm sorry it has to end this way, but you're right it's better than the way we've been acting. Only I'd hoped we could do it and keep some love and friendship, for our sakes and the children's."

"You've hoped a lot of things, Junior," she said bitterly, "but that's about the silliest. Good night. You can go back now to your drinks and your whore."

The line went dead.

150

"So," the Captain said, handing him his glass. "It's happened. Drink it, Arthur. You look as if you need it. How do you feel?"

"I don't know, Tom," he said. "Bewildered mainly, I guess. It's so sudden. After all that misery, I can't quite believe it."

"A little sad?"

"Sure I'm sad. It was a long time, Tom, and a lot of love and living went into it. You think she really means it?"

"Who knows what a woman means? You've got a lot of fighting to do yet, in the final settlement, but I think you've reached a turning point. You want to stay here tonight?"

"Don't be a fool," Arthur said, life returning in his grin. "Look, you really mean it about tomorrow?"

"Of course I mean it. I haven't looked forward to anything so much in years."

"Is there anything more we need to talk about?"

"Not a thing. I've got the picture. All I need is to get some sleep and show up bright and shining. That alone will confuse Henry enough to send us home free."

"Then I'll get on, Captain Carter," Arthur said, draining his glass. "I wouldn't want to interfere with your rest."

"Obliged," the Captain said. "But I do want to say one thing."

"Shoot."

"Just this," the Captain said, rolling himself to the cabinet and stowing the bottle and glasses. "When you tell Zelda tonight, you know, it's going to change things. A possibility has become a reality, Arthur, and if you back out on her after this, she'll never get over it. Don't tell her, Arthur, unless you know you mean it. If you do, she'll commit herself beyond the point of no return, and I would never forgive you if you left her there. I think, crippled as I am, I'd kill you. In fact, I know I would."

"I think you would too, Tom," Arthur said, holding out his hand. "And I'll tell you something else. I think you should. I'll never desert her, Tom. If you can depend on anything, you can depend on that. Do you believe me?"

"I believe you," the Captain said, taking Arthur's lean hand in his bony one. "I wouldn't have offered to come tomorrow if I hadn't. It was just a matter for the record, my boy. The eternal verities always bear repeating."

"And redoing," Arthur said, bending suddenly to kiss the

151

Captain's cold forehead. "God bless you, Tom. You don't know what you've done for me tonight."

"UnGod bless you," the Captain said, smiling as though the kiss had been a necessary ritual for any gentleman in such a circumstance, "and I appreciate that. You've become a good man, Arthur, and for Zelda's sake that means a great deal to me. Now will you go, or will I have to ask S. T. to evict you forcibly?"

"Don't use that whip, massa," Arthur said. "I'll go."

And bowed as the Captain's finger punched the buzzer, still almost in the center of the plateau.

20

Night. A darkness pale and unfulfilling, in which Zelda Huckaby battled desperately for oblivion. The humid air bathed her,
heavy on her nakedness. The moon filtered through the blinds,
spackling the carpet with a light that summoned her to wakefulness. Outside, summer noises, the unceasing life of the Georgia
night, mocked her futile efforts at denial.

God damn it, she had to sleep. She must be alert tomorrow,
ready for whatever evil Henry Maynard's impotent hatred might
devise. Clean and fresh, to hold herself inviolate in a battle they
were certain to lose. Especially now that her period had chosen
tonight to begin prematurely, a symptom of the tension it would
only intensify. What the hell did they all think she was, an iron
woman? Good old calm efficient Zelda, always smiling and relaxed, a hardboiled poor white bitch. Which tomorrow was precisely what, above all, she must seem to be.

Even to Arthur? That was the nub of it, damn it, the root
of all her uneasiness. Were they really there? Was he? What
prevailed now with Vicki, the certainty with which he had
mastered Henry and Ulysses, or the despair with which he had
greeted her only minutes before? Without her own assumption
of calm to sustain him, could he face disaster as the new man
he seemed to be? Was he his own man, or only hers, alive in a
partnership which failed him when they were no longer together? Could he bear to know that she also sometimes despaired?

And how about you, Zelda, she thought, how certain are you
of yourself? Are you really insisting on the wisdom, hard-won
in all the affairs in which you resisted total committment, of
accepting only a man who would demand in himself the honesty
without which your own soul will die? Or are you settling for an
acceptable substitute, deceiving yourself in the immemorial
fashion of widows and old maids, because you've tired of waiting
for what you've insisted on so long?

Honesty. Who the hell was she to talk about honesty? She'd
had it in love, more or less, but possibly, as any reasonably

stupid analyst would tell her, only because an incestuous passion for her father had blocked her off from anyone else. And yet she knew this was nonsense. Fred had been the man in her life, but as a symbol, not an obstacle. When Arthur took the final step across the line to total commitment, he would, she knew, consume her utterly.

But it wasn't Arthur she was thinking of. It was herself. And honesty. Her honesty, which was all she could do anything about. She remembered the night before Arthur had changed their plans for New Orleans, when she had sat brooding about the sham she had made of her life. Her bright, contained manner, calm and gay, which belied the passionate seriousness beneath. The house, which she had remade into a replica of her own facade, bright and modern and cheerful, even though she infinitely preferred it the way it had been in her father's day. And her attitude toward Arthur, warm and friendly, a good pal, to admit the final horror, denying the love she had lived by for years.

Well, she had voted to change that, resolved to lay herself bare, and that will do, Zelda, in New Orleans. As she had, but Arthur had been the one to take the initiative, thank God, so that she would never know what she might have done. Whatever it was, she was in nowise certain she would have liked it. She had resolved to seduce him, hadn't she, to persuade him, against all her principles, to take a step for which he was not yet ready? Or would she only have played it straight, revealing the truth she had denied, though he knew it, and accepting whatever happened? She doubted it. At least this was one discovery she had been spared.

So who cared? That was then, and their problem was now, in the courtroom, she found herself thinking and smiled at the image, in Henry Maynard's kangaroo trial around the Board table at the ass end of Arthur's office. And in the aftermath, the disaster which would be either their beginning or their end.

Shit. She couldn't sleep, wouldn't sleep, didn't want to sleep. The hell with it. It was all wrong anyway, trying to bury herself in rest and respectability, to husband, to coin the wrong phrase, her resources so that she could face Henry Maynard on his own terms. She'd have to do it her own way. When she was ready, sleep would come. If not, she would depend on the vitality that had never failed her. And fuck little Henry. Let's have a drink.

She got up lightly, slipped on a robe, and went down to the kitchen. She was wrestling with the ice tray, stuck as usual, when the doorbell rang. Now who the hell would that be, she thought. It wouldn't be Arthur, not tonight, and nothing else could be good news. Fear gripped her as she went out to peer through the glass. That woman was capable of anything, and this wasn't the night she could take it.

It was Arthur, grinning stupidly in the sudden light.

"Darling," she cried, struggling with chains and nightlatches that refused to loosen, all the paraphernalia of a woman's non-existent safety, "darling, darling, goddamn these locks, O come in, come in."

She threw herself on him, burying her face against his damp shirt while he kissed her hair.

"Oh, baby," she said, "you couldn't sleep either? I know I shouldn't be glad, but I am. God, I needed you so, but I never thought you'd come. Not tonight."

"I came all right, honey," he said, opening her robe to hold her naked against him. "In fact, I came for good. If you'll have me."

"What do you mean?" she said, looking up at him. "This is no night for jokes."

"I mean Vicki and I are finished. Kaput. We've agreed to separate."

"Agreed? How?"

"I came home and found her drunk and we had another terrible fight. She passed out and I put her to bed and went over to Captain Tom's. I'll tell you about that later, it's important. A little while ago, Vicki called up and asked me again to leave you. I said *no*, and we agreed that that was that. So here I am."

"You mean you left because *she* asked you to?"

"Now look, goddam it," Arthur said, pushing the door to and turning her toward the kitchen, "don't sound like Vicki. Not tonight. Have you any idea how many times she's pleaded with me to give you up? Or the kind of pressures that's been on me, the kind of hell I've been through every time I said *no*? You know what I've been trying to do. Settle this reasonably for the children's sakes. So when she finally got around to saying *either*,

155

or, I said *or*. Jesus, Zelda, isn't that good enough for you? I thought you'd be happy."

"Oh, darling," she said, stifling the last small doubt, "I am happy. You don't know how happy. I know this seems foolish to you, Arthur, but I have to know you're doing this for yourself. Not because Vicki decided it. Can you understand that?"

"Sure I understand it. But can't you see it's true? How the hell do you think we got here except that I've been so damned insistent that she and I were finished and you and I were it for good? Would you rather have had me just kick them all in the ass and leave?"

"No, darling," she said, "of course I wouldn't. I wouldn't want you to be heartless. The fact that you care about other people, the way you're always thoughtful of people at the Henhouse, that's part of my loving you. It's just that—oh, hell, fix us a drink, will you, and I'll try to explain. I'd just gotten up and was fighting that damned ice tray when you rang."

"All right," he said, freeing the tray with a practiced hand, "it's a deal. Even though I've got news for you, Zelda. Nothing needs explaining any more. But go ahead."

"It's this," Zelda said, sitting down at the table where they had never breakfasted. "You know I'm a woman, Arthur, God knows you've had a chance to find that out, but I'm not sure you realize I'm an imperfect one. Or maybe I mean to say a good one. I'm not always gay and cheerful, and I don't want to have to be with you. I get depressed, and I want to be able to show it. I get afraid, maybe for no reason, like tonight, wondering what would happen to us after the show is over tomorrow. Sometimes I'm irrational. Jesus, Arthur, I understand the way Vicki's been acting. I don't respect her for it, and I have no use for the destroying part that comes from hate, but I understand fear and the irrationality that comes from it, and I know that in her because I've been there myself. Most of all, darling, for us, I get afraid when I wonder whether you're fully commited. If I was irrational, that's why. Can you understand that?"

"Baby," he said, handing her a drink and sitting down beside her, "I've got news for you. I understand perfectly. And I've got a confession. A little while ago I wouldn't have understood at all. But now it's very simple. We're stuck, Zel. Together, permanently, and for good. Nothing else matters, and not a

156

goddamn thing has to be explained. That's it, all of it. Can *you* understand that?"

"Oh, Arthur," she said, her face collapsing as it once had in the Henhouse, eternities ago, "do you really mean it? Do you know what you're saying?"

"I know exactly what I'm saying," he said, his hand on her breast. "I mean I take you just as you are, all of you, and you do the same with me. And no questions. As naturally as I do this tit," which he bent to suck, "and for good. Is that clear?"

"Jesus, yes," she said, bringing his head to her other breast. "Kiss me and then tell me about Tom, quick so we can get to bed."

"All right," he said, "though I don't like being interrupted at my work. It's marvelous, Zel. You know what he's going to do?"

"Of course I don't, damn it. Tell me."

"He's going to defend us at the Board meeting."

"Tom? Will they let him in?"

"They can't help it. Don't you read our stationery? He's a member."

"You mean that's on the level? It isn't just honorary?"

"Legal and all the way. He's got as much right there as anybody else."

"But will he be there? Sober?"

"He'll be there, bright-eyed and bushy tailed. And he'll knock Henry Maynard on his ass."

"But honey, that's wonderful. You mean you think we have a chance?"

"Chance? I know damned well we'll win. And get a new chairman to boot. How do you like that?"

"I like it just fine," she said, dropping her robe as she rose. "But there are other things I'm going to like even better. Come on."

"Roger," he said. "But I hope when we're married it won't take you so damned long to get to bed."

"Not if you're always sure you love me," she said, pulling him behind her. "Come on."

"Now look," he said, holding her back. "One more stupid remark and I'm going to kick you square in the ass. Understand?"

"Roger to you," she said, turning away. Suddenly she stopped.

157

"Oh, honey, I forgot. My period began tonight. If you don't—"

His foot caught her square on the right buttock, spinning her around into his arms.

"Understand?" he said.

"Yes, master," she said, shock fading into love, and they moved arm in arm toward the stairs.

21

It was three in the morning when Vicki ripped off the sheet.

They lay locked on the blood-stained bed, his leg between hers, one arm beneath her neck, the other across her outstretched palm, her left arm curled protectively around his naked back. A beast with two backs and joined limbs, slumbering and satiate.

"You see, Margie," Vicki hissed, "you see what your father has taken up with? An animal that ruts in her period like a bitch in heat. You see why I'm so upset? Look at them. Look. I want you to never forget it. I want you to remember it every time I'm unhappy, so you'll know what this whore has done to us."

Arthur, blinking in the hard sudden light, wakened to see his oldest daughter at the foot of the bed, her face alive with fascination and horror, held fast by Vicki, whose eyes were bright with madness.

"Goddamn it, Vicki," he said, sitting up, "what are you doing here? And what the hell's the idea of bringing Margie? Are you out of your mind?"

"I wanted her to learn," Vicki said coldly. "I wanted her to see a whore so she'll know what not to be."

"I'm sorry, Marj," Arthur said gently, "I'm sorry you had to be exposed to this, darling."

At her old nickname, the symbol of their lost intimacy, the girl began to blubber softly.

"Let's go now, mother," she said, burying her face in her hands, "please let's go now, please mother, please."

"You heard her, Vicki," Arthur said, getting out of bed. "Now get going."

"I'll get going when I'm good and ready," Vicki said. "She's *my* daughter, now that you've deserted us for this whore. And don't you dare touch me, Arthur Evans. I'll call the police. Adultery is a criminal offense in this state, in case you didn't know."

"And so is breaking and entering," Zelda said, coming around the other side of the bed. "This is my house, Vicki, and before I call the cops I'm asking you politely to get out."

"Please," Margie sobbed, cringing as Zelda came close to her, "please mother, *please* let's go."

"*You'll* call the police?" Vicki said scornfully. "And let the whole town know you've been whoring with my husband? I thought even you had more sense than that."

"Don't cry, darling," Arthur said, going around to take his daughter in his arms. "Don't worry, Marj. It'll be all right."

"I don't give a damn what this town thinks," Zelda said, "but you do. If you want them to know you were cruel enough to bring this poor child here, it's your worry, not mine."

"You wouldn't dare," Vicki said. "Even you wouldn't be that low, you cheap bitch."

"Okay," Zelda said, turning toward the door. "And how would you like to kiss my rosy, poor white ass?"

"You heard her, Arthur," Vicki said, clutching his arm. "You heard what she said to me. That's the kind of woman you've got, who'd talk like that to your own wife."

"Please, daddy," Margie said, putting her arms around his neck. "I can't stand it. Please make her go."

"All right, Vicki," Arthur said. "You heard her. Do you go now, or do I have to throw you out?"

"You take your hands off that child," Vicki said, her eyes blazing at him. "You'll be trying to seduce her next, you lecher. You haven't even got the decency to cover yourself in front of your daughter."

"That's enough," Arthur said, freeing Margie's arms and advancing toward Vicki. "Out!"

"Oh, God," Margie said, and ran, blindly past Zelda, who stood waiting quietly behind them, desperately through the liberating door.

"Out," Arthur said, turning Vicki around and shoving her after Margie. "Catch her, you fool."

"Don't touch me!" Vicki screamed, already in motion, running with her familiar sway, feet slightly splayed as she plunged frantically down the stairs, Arthur pounding his feet in mock pursuit. Seconds after the screen door slammed her engine fired, and tires spattered gravel as the car roared away. When the tail lights had veered into the night, Arthur secured all the locks and went slowly back upstairs.

"Well?" he said, coming slowly over to Zelda, who still stood quietly by the door.

"Well?" she said, putting her arms around him.

"Let's go to bed," he said. "We need to be ready for to-morrow."

They kissed ,and curled together on the bloody sheets.

22

"He does not," Henry Maynard said. "I won't stand for it."

"But you have to stand for it, Henry," Arthur said cheerfully. "There's nothing to argue about. Tom is a member of this Board in good standing, legally qualified in exactly the same fashion as the rest of you, and if he is willing to make the effort to be with us on the occasion of this special meeting, I for one think your remark is in very poor taste."

The Board was assembled, shirt-sleeved, except for Henry Maynard, in the August heat, their coats neatly hung in the closet sanctified to this purpose. Despite their increasing use in Phoenix offices, air conditioners, in sturdy deference to the tradition of Henhouse austerity, were not employed at Taliaferro Institute for the Blind.

The members had arrived in their usual fashion, Henry making his polite and chilly entrance precisely on the dot of ten, the others drifting casually in during the fifteen minute grace period which was a staple of Phoenix mores, six tried men and true who had for twenty years ruled in such harmony that it had never occurred to anyone that their perpetually missing seventh need be replaced, who had barely time to observe the empty space at Arthur's side before Tom Carter swept onstage in regal splendor.

"Now don't you worry none, Captain Tom," S. T. had said, poised and catlike at the helm of the wheelchair, "I'll have you in there by Mr. Arthur so slick these gentlemen all wish they had a chair as comfortable too."

And had, bowing politely out when his cargo was deposited, leaving the Captain, clear-eyed and hearty, to smile genially at his colleagues.

"Delighted to see you looking so well this morning, Henry," he had said, "and you Doc, and Floyd and Frank and George and Joe. Mighty fine to be here with you."

"A pleasure to have you, Tom," Henry had said uncertainly. "To what do we owe the honor?"

"A duty long neglected for which I would make recompense. Hearing that there are matters to be decided this morning of grave importance to the institution for which we are jointly responsible, I bestirred myself, as I confess I have not during years of more routine foregatherings, to take my place in your deliberations and contribute, in such small measure I can, to the solution of these difficulties."

"I'm sure we're all grateful, Tom. Considering, I mean, the trouble it must have caused you. We will certainly be pleased to hear any comments you might care to make."

"That wasn't exactly what I had in mind, Henry," the Captain said, dropping grandiloquence. "And just for future reference, you might keep in mind that no cripple likes to hear his handicap referred to quite so openly. No, I didn't come to advise, Henry. I came to vote."

"Vote?" Henry said, coloring at the rebuke. "Surely you're joking."

"I was never more serious in my life."

"As President and Secretary," Arthur said, "I should perhaps point out that, under the by-laws, although he has not generally attended our meetings, he has the same voting power as any other member."

At which Henry Maynard had exploded.

"I didn't mean it that way," he was saying now. "I just meant that a man who hasn't attended a meeting for twenty years is hardly qualified to vote on a basic policy question which may determine the future of the Institution."

"Precisely why I am here," the Captain said. "And I accept your apology, Henry, grudging though it may be. I take it what you mean to say is that I am out of touch with goings on here at the Henhouse. Mind if I ask you a few questions?"

"I hardly see the relevance, but it's your privilege."

"What are the names of Ulysses Futral's three chief assistants, Henry?"

"Surely you don't expect me to bother with details like that."

"I could tell you. But suppose we shift to something basic. How many writers have we sold in each of the past five years?"

"Why, it's in the records, Tom," Henry Maynard said, the grim line growing grimmer. "I don't carry the figures in my head."

"I do. How about the Ohio modification, Henry? Precisely

163

what does it do, and why was it important for us to adopt it?"

"I'm not so sure it was the right thing for us to do. It's made a lot of trouble."

"What kind of trouble?"

"Well, there's that part, and —"

"The one that wasn't deburred? I spoke to Ulysses this morning, and he tells me that now that he's had them buffed everything's working like a charm. What else?"

"Now look here," Henry said hotly, "we've had enough of this nonsense. It's time this meeting came to order, and as Chairman of the Board I rule that Captain Tom Carter, though a welcome guest, is not legally entitled to a vote."

"Now just a minute, Henry," Frank Newton said in his deliberate lawyer's voice. "You're chairman, all right, but you ain't the by-laws. As I read these, there's not the slightest doubt that members of this Board hold office until officially removed, and to my certain knowledge no one has ever even suggested that Tom be disqualified. I for one am delighted to see him here today, and I respect the dedication that brought him here to cast his vote."

"Second," Floyd Butler said. "What's all the fuss about, Henry?"

"There's no fuss," Henry said desperately. "I just like to have things regular, that's all. If you gentlemen have no objection, by all means let Tom vote. Now can we get on with the business of the meeting?"

"Indeed," the Captain said. "To this end I move that we dispense with the regular agenda and proceed directly to new business."

"Second," said Floyd Butler.

"All in favor," Henry said mechanically, the earth moving under his feet. "The ayes have it."

"All right then, Henry," the Captain said cheerfully. "Suppose you tell us what this is all about."

Henry glared at him, and Tom resisted a temptation to stick out his tongue, contenting himself with a judicious stroking of the unfamiliar arm of his traveling chair.

"As most of you already know," Henry began at last, "we are here to consider a serious charge, malfeasance, against our President, Arthur Evans."

"Malfeasance?" the Captain said, interested. "Of course you don't mean misfeasance."

"Misfeasance?" said Henry, off the rails again.

"Often confused. Malfeasance, wrong-doing, specifically official wrong-doing. Misfeasance, doing the right thing in the wrong way. Just means you don't like the way he went about it. But of course you have evidence he wasn't doing his job properly. Official misconduct, that is."

"I'll say it's official misconduct. Adultery with a fellow employee, Zelda Huckaby. I don't see how misconduct could get much worse."

"Adultery?" the Captain said, musing. "I always had an idea that was a rather private affair. You mean to say they've been doing it right here in the Henhouse?"

George Shepherd laughed, and Henry rewarded him with a glare like those he reserved for the Captain.

"I don't see what's so funny about it," Henry said. "If you'll stop trying to turn this into a circus, Tom, maybe we can get on to considering the effect of such conduct on the Institution for which we are responsible.

"Now wait a minute, Henry," the Captain said calmly, "let's not get our dander up. Like you, I'm only trying to keep things regular. If the charge is malfeasance, I would like to know how this relationship, as yet unsubstantiated —"

"It's substantiated, all right," Henry cut in. "It's the talk of the whole place."

"Curious," the Captain said reflectively, "I didn't hear anything about it this morning, and I've been gossiping around back there since nine o'clock. But perhaps you have more reliable sources of information. Henry. Tell us about them."

"Never mind my sources," Henry said angrily. "How do you suppose I heard of it if there wasn't talk?"

"That's just what I'm curious about, Henry. How *did* you get this so-called information? I'm sure we'd all like to know."

"None of your business," Henry said, his voice shrilling. "I don't have to explain to you, Tom Carter. The point is, what are we going to do about it?"

"Now just a minute, Henry," Joe Cheatham said in the bass rumble he cultivated to camoflauge his youth. "I'm afraid you do have to explain. You can't prefer charges like this without backing them up. Suppose you tell us exactly why and how you came to believe that this alleged relationship existed, and your reasons for believing that it was sufficiently prejudicial to the Institute to warrant this extraordinary session. Speaking for myself, I must say you led me to expect something considerably more lurid than has so far appeared when you called me yesterday afternoon."

"Very well," Henry said, shifting in his chair. "Ulysses Futral called me the other night and said it was urgent that he talk to me. He was very upset. I told him to come over, and he told me about this shameful business. Said it was ruining the morale of the Institute and he felt it was his duty to report it."

"You might also add," the Captain said, "that Ulysses did not just happen to call you. He's been spying for you for some time, and you've conferred on several previous occasions about ways to sabotage the Ohio modification."

"That's not true!" Henry shouted. "I demand you withdraw that."

"You mean you deny you had Ulysses over? I can prove it."

"I mean your shameful allegation that I was attempting to sabotage the Institute. As was my duty as Chairman of the Board, I listened to complaints brought to me by a responsible employee."

"Behind the backs of the Board and the President," the Captain said calmly, "and without ever reporting to them. However, we'll get to that. Do I understand that Ulysses' story was your sole source of information? An employee whom we know to have been gravely dissatisfied with the new policy Mr. Evans had instituted?"

"Indeed not," Henry said grimly. "On the following day I came to the Institute and conferred with Mr. Evans and Miss Huckaby. This interview convinced me the allegations were correct, and accordingly I called this meeting. For all practical purposes, they admitted it."

"What Arthur told you, to refresh your memory, was that, as you so elegantly said to me a moment ago, it was none of your business. That your sole responsibility was to estimate their value as employees of the Institute, and that in fact the events you witnessed that morning amply demonstrated what you should have known already, that they were invaluable."

166

"I must say, Tom," Floyd Butler said, stroking his ample belly, "for a man who's been off the scene so long you're remarkably well informed. Much more so than the rest of us. I'd appreciate it if one of you would explain more about this meeting yesterday."

"In due time, Floyd," the Captain said, grinning. "As for being informed, I make it my business to be. It's all I've got left in life. But to return to the question. The charge against our President is malfeasance. The only relevance of this alleged relationship —"

"Alleged, hell," Henry shouted. "I even talked to his wife yesterday. She was in tears about this dreadful business."

"You've been a remarkably thorough snoop, Henry," the Captain said admiringly, "even though your language is deplorable for a Chairman of the Board. I'm disappointed you haven't favored us with a report from Zelda's maid. However, let's try to stick to the question. The only evidence you have adduced that this relationship might be harmful to Mr. Evans' work is the statement made to you by Ulysses that it was damaging the morale of the Institution. Perhaps it would be advisable to pursue this point."

"Now you're talking sense, Tom," Doc said. "Let's call Ulysses in and ask him."

"I don't think that will be necessary, Doc," the Captain said. "He's busy, and it would only upset him. It happens I have a statement on the matter from Ulysses, prepared and signed by him this morning. After you have heard it, if it is our desire to question him further, we can do so. Will you read this, Henry, or shall I?"

"Doesn't matter," Henry said. "Be a pack of lies anyway."

"A curious comment," the Captain said, "about a man who a few minutes ago was your principal witness. However. Is it the sense of the meeting that I proceed with the statement?"

"Read it," Floyd Butler said. "This thing's starting to get me curious."

"Very well," the Captain said, taking a paper out of his inside pocket and putting on his reading glasses. "It's in Ulysses' own hand, as you can observe when I pass it around afterwards. 'I, Ulysses Futral,' it begins, 'wish to make the following statement. I had no cause to tell Mr. Maynard there was anything wrong

167

between Mr. Arthur and Miss Zelda. I never seen nothing except they liked each other and liked to work together. I made it up to make trouble, because I wanted to get rid of the Ohio modification, same reason as I talked to Mr. Maynard before and had someone call Mr. Evans' wife and tell her lies too. I was wrong and Mr. Evans was right. I've told him I'm sorry, and I hope he'll let me keep on making writers. The modified writer is better than the old one. Signed, Ulysses Futral.' "

There was a long silence.

"Well, Henry," Frank Newton said at last, "what do you say to that?"

"There's nothing to say," Henry said, his face ashen, "nothing you'd believe anyway. They're doing the same kind of job on you I saw them do on Ulysses, the kind they've obviously already done on Tom, and nothing I could say would convince you."

"Nobody's done any job on me, Henry," the Captain said dangerously, "and I don't propose to let you start. As for convincing, I'd say the facts are doing that. Suppose you tell us what you mean."

"I mean," said Henry, his voice rising again, "that these two are the biggest con artists that ever hit this town. Can't you see the way they're pulling the wool over your eyes? If you knew what they were really like, you'd never let them inside the Institute."

"I think that's about enough of that kind of talk, Henry," Frank Newton said. "We've had plenty of unsupported accusations for one day. Arthur, would you mind telling us what went on at that meeting that Henry keeps referring to?"

"Glad to, Frank," Arthur said. "It's not very complicated. I managed to convince Ulysses that I knew more about some of these problems than he did, such as what was wrong with the new part, and to let him know he could depend on me. Then he levelled with me about what he'd been doing, and apologized. Ulysses is a good old fellow, really, and he didn't want to be acting the way he was. He was just upset because I was changing the way he'd done things for thirty years, and he was scared. People do funny things when they're afraid, but it's all right right now. Zelda has a complete transcript of everything that was said during that meeting, by the way, if you'd like to hear it."

168

"Another cheap trick," Henry said. "She was taking notes all the time when I didn't even know about it."

"That's about enough out of you, Henry," Floyd Butler said, flexing his great arms on the table. "If Arthur doesn't give you a poke in the nose, as I admire him for not having done yet, I'm likely to do it myself. Now shut up. Gentlemen, I think we've heard about enough. Who wants to make a motion of confidence in our President?"

"There's just one thing," Joe Cheatham said, "and now that we've got the cards on the table I think we'd better look at it. Arthur, believe me, I'm not prying into your business, but if there's going to be a scandal, which is part of what Henry had in mind, I'm sure, it might affect the Institute. Now that we've gone this far, I think we have a responsibility to consider it."

"I'd like to speak to that, Joe," the Captain said, quieting Arthur with a hand on his arm, "and then after we have our motion I've got another one to make myself. If I could stand up to say what I'm going to now, gentlemen, I would, because I'd like it to be eloquent. Every one of us has scandals in his past. I know some of yours, and you know some of mine. This very Institution had its beginning in a scandalous accident. It's hot blooded country down here, and what you call scandal, Joe, is a part of the web of our life. But we've never let it interfere with a good man's getting a job done, *not* unless it interferes with the job. I don't know you very well, Joe, but your father and your granfather were partners of mine, kept our firm going back in the depression when I didn't do much more than moon around. I'd be surprised if you hadn't inherited their common sense. Therefore, boy, the way I'd answer your question is this. If something happens, at some time in the future, which affects the business or good name of the Institute, then it will be our responsibility as trustees to consider it. But until something does, we've no damned business meddling in anybody's private affairs."

"Hear, hear," George Shepherd said. "Mr. Chairman, I move that this Board express its full confidence in our President, Mr. Arthur Evans."

"Second," said Floyd Butler.

"All in favor," said Henry Maynard listlessly. "The ayes have it. There being no further new business, gentlemen —"

"I have further business," the Captain said.

"What is it?"

"It'll take a little time. Arthur, what do the by-laws say about the term of the Chairman of the Board?"

"He serves at the convenience of the Board."

"Very well, then. Gentlemen, I would like to move that Henry Maynard be relieved of his duties as Chairman of the Board, effective immediately. My grounds are that his charges against our President were motivated by malice and personal spite. If one of you will scond my motion, I'll be glad to present my evidence."

"Second," said Floyd Butler.

"This is absolutely out of order," Henry said, the enormity of the challenge rallying him to the attack. "Tom Carter coming in here after twenty years and trying to upset the whole structure of the Board. It's unheard of."

"It's absolutely in order, Henry," Frank Newton said. "The motion has been legally made and seconded. It would also be in order for you to relieve yourself of the chair while a motion involving you is being discussed."

"All right," Henry said, after a long look around the ring of faces. "Joe, I appoint you Chairman pro tem."

"Very well," Joe said, as brisk as his rumble would allow. "What evidence did you wish to present, Tom?"

"Will you ask Zelda to come in, Arthur," the Captain said, "and bring the transcript of yesterday's meeting?"

"This is nonsense," Henry said indignantly. "It's just another of their tricks. Can't you see it's just their word against mine?"

"That's your line in the script, Henry," the Captain said. "You don't have to repeat it. As for evidence, I've taken the precaution of having Ulysses read the sections including him, which constitute the largest part of the record, and I have another note from him, which I will now pass around, affirming that it is, in his belief, entirely accurate. I am confident the Board will accept the accuracy of the remainder. Ah yes, my dear. Come in."

She entered gracefully, poised and beautiful, and took her place between the Captain and Arthur.

"I won't bother with formalities, Zelda," the Captain said. "You know all these gentlemen and you are aware of the purpose of the meeting. I do think you should know that the Board has

170

voted complete confidence in Arthur as President and we are now considering a motion to relieve Henry Maynard of the Chairmanship."

Her heart flickered briefly in her eyes, but she remained silent.

"What I would like you to do," the Captain said, "is read from the record of yesterday's meeting."

"From the beginning?"

"No, skip the part with Ulysses. Begin where Henry finds out you're making notes."

" 'Notes.' " she read. " 'Do you mean you're making a record of this, Zelda? That's an invasion of privacy.'

" 'Not just *a* record, Henry. A complete stenographic record. Every word. Among other things, Zelda is an excellent secretary.'

" 'Katherine Gibbs, forty-two. I don't miss a word, Henry.'

" 'What's the point of a trick like this?'

" 'It's no trick, Henry. Just a precaution, in case you're planning the kind of trouble I think you are. Something to read at the next Board meeting.'

" 'It would just be your word against mine.' "

At the hated phrase, Henry reddened and glared angrily at Arthur, but Zelda read steadily on, the Board listening intently and in silence.

"One *l* in bullshit, Arthur?" she read, and the silence broke. Led by George Shepherd, whose whoop set off the explosion, the Board relieved itself in laughter, dissipating its tensions in an orgy of joyless mirth.

"That's enough," Henry Maynard keened, erect in his place, a pathetic dignity mantling his crumpled face and store-bought elegance. "I will not stay to be mocked by colleagues whom I once respected. You have my resignation, gentlemen, and I wish you the joy of finding, too late, that you would have done well to heed my warnings."

He turned and strode quickly out of the office, slamming the door behind him.

"Too bad," Frank Newton said. "I guess we shouldn't have laughed like that."

"Leave us not get carried away by Henry's exit," the Captain said. "After all this misery, how could we help taking the first laugh anybody's handed us? Anyway, I don't forget the

171

Henry we just heard in this transcript, or the way he conducted himself during the meeting."

"Nor I," Floyd Butler said. "Who makes the motion we accept his resignation?"

"I so move," George Shepherd said.

"Second," said Floyd Butler.

"Discussion?" Joe Cheatham said. "No? All in favor? The ayes have it. Shall we proceed to elect a new Chairman?"

"Let's table it," Frank Newton said. "We've had enough today. Let's give ourselves time to think things over. Need a new Board member too, and we ought to settle that before we elect a chairman."

"Roger," Joe Cheatham said. "Unless I hear a contrary motion I'll consider it the sense of the meeting. Motion to adjourn?"

"I'd like to make a statement," Arthur said, rising.

"Go ahead," Joe said. "I should have asked you."

"First I want to thank you for your vote of confidence," Arthur said. "I accept it because I think that in the last few months I've earned it. I'd be the first to admit that until recenly mine has been prety much a caretaker's administration, but I'm proud of having carried through the modification of our writer. This will be a service to blind people all over the country, and it's one thing I'll be glad to have on my tombstone, a landmark in a generally undistinguished life. A life, however, that is changing."

He smiled down at Zelda, took a sip of water, and continued.

"However, I don't wish to accept your confidence under false pretenses. I'm sure it's clear from the record Zelda read you that I feel rather strongly that people's private lives, including mine, are their own. I'm sorry you missed the story that follows, since it's one of my favorites, but thinking now, I'm going to see that each of you gets a full transcript, since it will also show you that the reason Henry called this meeting was that Zelda had the drop on him on Mae Snider. But what I wanted to say is this, and I tell you not because anyone asked it, but out of my own free will, because I want you to hear it straight from me."

He paused, placing his hands on the table and looking around at them.

"It is utterly false that there has been any relationship be-

172

tween Zelda Huckaby and myself that involved the Henhouse or affected it or our work. It is true, however, that I am in love with her, that I have separated from my wife and will be divorced from her, and that Zelda and I will be married. This, as I have said, is my own business. If it disturbs you gentlemen, however, you may have my resignation on request at any time, including this morning. If you would like to discuss this privately, Zelda and I will be glad to leave the room. I would like to say first, though, how much I appreciate the cooperation and help this board has always given me, not only this morning but for the past seventeen years. Thank you."

"Thank you," Joe said, after Arthur had sat down into a loud silence, "I'm sure we all appreciate your frankness. What's your pleasure, gentlemen? Do you wish to go into executive session?"

"I don't see how that's necessary," Frank Andrews said deliberately, after a look at Floyd Butler. "Arthur has laid his cards on the table, and so have we. Unless there is an opinion to the contrary, I would say we had already disposed of the matter by prior vote."

"Further discussion?" Joe said, hopefully, it seemed to Arthur. "No? Motion to adjourn? George? All in favor? Adjourned."

They rose, dissolving into the nervous smalltalk that follows unpleasant decisions. In a show of seemly hesitation they retrieved their coats from the closet, stopped for a smiling word with Arthur and Zelda, and hurried off to urgent business. Only Doc hung back a moment, to wink at Arthur and kiss Zelda on the cheek.

"Great show, Tom," he said. "By God, I was proud of you. And I was proud of you too, Arthur. You laid it on the line."

When they were alone, Zelda kissed Arthur full on the mouth, caressing him with eyes brimming with pride and love, and then wrapped her arms around the Captain's neck and kissed his bald spot.

"Darling," she said, "I still don't believe it. How in hell did you carry it off?"

"By being the meanest man in town," the Captain said. "Ask Henry. It's easy if you've had practice. But how about Arthur? That took guts, boy, and I salute you. But also, friend, I hope that you have not abandoned the custom, wisely initiated by your predecessors, of keeping a small tot of medicinal alcohol on the premises."

"And ice," Arthur said, extracting mixings from a cabinet. "I knew we'd be drinking to something, Tom, but I wasn't sure it wouldn't be the past."

"As we yet will be," the Captain said, accepting the glass. "We only won round one, and the next meeting will be a different story. Wait till the scandal starts. Young Joe Cheatham, that respectable horse's ass, speaks for the new Phoenix, and Joe Cheatham is worried. So are the others, even though they backed you. Remember what I told you at the beginning, Arthur. Phoenix won't forgive you for Zelda. Don't let this morning fool you. Be ready for anything, boy, and remember they don't show their teeth just to smile. As Oliver Whittlesby used to remark, or maybe it was Confucius, shark fighters make lousy golfers. They lose too many balls."

"Oh, shame on both of you," Zelda said. "You were wonderful, and I'm damned if we're going to waste time worrying about tomorrow. Let's toast now to a wonderful day."

"And night," Arthur said. "Your health, Tom. And thanks."

"Yours, children," the Captain said. "But I should be the one to thank you. In the parlance of Margie's generation, Arthur, I had a ball."

23

While they celebrated their dubious victory, Margie summoned up the courage to speak to Vicki at last.

"Mother," she said, coming into the bedroom where Vicki lay brooding on clean striped sheets, "I've got to talk to you."

"About last night, you mean?" Vicki said, turning her head languidly toward her oldest daughter, her damp curls flaccid on the rumpled pillow, her body slack beneath the nightgown which, for the first time in Margie's memory, she had not bothered to change before coming downstairs.

It was the nightgown, more than anything else, that had kept Margie from talking to her after breakfast. She had resolved to last night, driving home silently from the scene that had terrified and freed her. What right had they to be sanctimonious about her when they got themselves into messes like that? Those awful sheets, and father with blood on his cock.

She felt like laughing, only it wasn't funny at all, God if she could be like that now she'd have Freddy all over her and kiss him afterwards, only he wouldn't have sense enough to do it then, the fool, he'd think it wasn't clean. At least she'd learned that much. People did it, no matter what the books said. And from the way they acted, it must have been fun. She wondered if it felt any different.

Parents were so awful. Mother now, acting like she owned all the trouble in the world, coming down in that nightgown and an old robe like she couldn't bear to turn loose her misery for a second. Not even long enough to listen to a daughter with real trouble and then coming back up to bed. Well, she'd have to now. That's what parents were for, wasn't it, to help you when you were in trouble. God knows they talked about it enough.

"Not exactly," she said now. "About something else."

"Then that can wait," Vicki said, not moving. "I want to explain to you about last night. You do understand, don't you, why I had to take you there? You had to see, dear, so you could understand, you had to know that thing for what she is, so you'll know what we have to do to help your father come to his senses. I'm sorry it upset you last night, but in the long run you'll be glad."

"Yes, mother," Margie said absently. "Look. There's something I've got to tell you."

"You don't act as if you heard me," Vicki said. "Don't give me that absent-minded routine, Margie. Did you understand what I said to you?"

"I understand, mother, but you've got to listen. This is important."

"More important than your father's running off with that cheap whore?"

"It is to me. I'm knocked up, mother. I'm two months pregnant."

"You're *what?*" Vicki said, sitting up and pulling her daughter down beside her. "Are you sure?"

"Yes, I'm sure," Margie said, beginning to cry now that there was no longer any need to pretend. "I've missed my last two periods."

"Who was it?"

"Freddy Maynard."

"How do you know?"

"Because he's the only one I ever do it with. Anyway I know just when it happened."

"You knew, and you let it happen anyway?"

"I don't see you've got anything to brag about," Margie said resentfully. "None of you looked so smart last night."

"When did it happen?" Vicki said, ignoring her.

"In Freddy's car, just before my period was due. He didn't have anything, and it was so close we thought it was all right, so we did it. And then I never fell off the roof. Not last month either."

"When are you due again?"

"Right now. But nothing's going to happen, mother," she said fiercely. "I'm pregnant. I know it. I can feel things beginning to change. My breasts are sore if I lie on them at night."

"Have you told Freddy?"

"Yes."

"What does he want to do?"

"He wants to get rid of it."

176

"What do you want to do?"

"I want to get married. Lots of the kids are. We could have fun."

"Do you love him?"

"As much as anybody. We have a good enough time."

"Does he love you?"

"More than I do him. He doesn't want to let me go. He just thinks he'll be free and that he'll have me anyway. He'll get over that after we're married. I can handle Freddy."

"All right," Vicki said, "I won't waste time bawling you out, even though I ought to. But why didn't you talk to me, you damned little fool? I'd have taken you to Atlanta and bought you a diaphragm."

"Why didn't you talk to me?" Margie said resentfully. "How was I to know you'd take it like that? You're my mother. It's up to you to teach me the facts of life."

"Don't be fresh," Vicki said automatically. "Are you sure you want to marry him?"

"I don't have too many choices, do I?"

"You could have an abortion."

"*No*," Margie said, beginning to cry again. "I won't let you take my baby from me. It's mine, and I'm going to have it. Besides, I'd probably end up marrying Freddy anyway, there's nobody else around here that really suits either of us, and if I had an abortion we'd never be able to face each other again. I'd hate him, and I don't want that. I'd hate you too, for making me do it, and I'd never let you forget it."

"But what about college? When you go away from here you might meet somebody else, somebody you *really* liked. Oh honey, you're so young. Are you sure you want to tie yourself down now?"

"Somebody I really liked like you did Daddy?" Margie said scornfully. "Look at where it got you. You think I didn't know why he took up with that woman? You've been giving him a hard time for years. Freddy and I'll take our chances now. Even if it doesn't work out, we'll have had fun. I *like* doing it, mommy. I want to do it every night. I want to do it in my own bed. I want my own house. I want my own baby. You've got to help me, mommy. You've got to, or I'll die."

"If you want my help, you'd better not talk like that," Vicki

177

said, trapped in anger and self-pity. "Shame on you for saying I gave your father a hard time. He couldn't ask for a better wife than I've been, and you know it. Who do you think's worried about you all these years when your father was out doing God knows what? Who's looking after you now when he's off with that whore? You'd better figure out which side your bread's buttered on, Margie, and keep a civil tongue in your head. Coming in here after disgracing yourself and then talking to your own mother like that."

"I'll talk the way I want to," Margie said desperately. "You never loved me anyway. All you ever did was boss me around. Daddy's the only one ever loved me, and now I've lost him because he had to find another woman who'd be nice to him. He's the only one paid any attention to me last night. You didn't care any more about me than she did. If you don't want to help me, don't. I'll go to Daddy. He won't let me down."

"Stop it!" Vicki said, panic stricken, seizing Margie as she started to rise from the bed. "You don't know what you're saying, baby. We're both upset, and we're just saying things to hurt each other. You know I love you, baby. You're my little girl, and I'll do anything for you. Anything. Of course I'll help you. I'll talk to Henry Maynard later today, and we'll see that Freddy marries you. Henry wants it too, I know. There won't be any trouble. We'll have a big church wedding with all the trimmings, and if anyone wonders when the baby's born we'll tell them premature babies run in the family."

"You mean it, Mommy?" Margie said, smiling through her tears. "You really mean it?"

"Of course I mean it," Vicki said, kissing her. "You didn't think your mother would let you down, did you?"

"A church wedding," Margie said. "With candles and everything. And our own apartment. I don't care what they say after that, Mommy. I don't care who wonders about the baby's being early. I'll just do like Daddy always says, and shut my mouth and tell them to go to hell inside me. It happens all the time. There's nothing wrong with it as long as the baby's born in wedlock."

"Of course there isn't, baby," Vicki said, gentling her hair. "I'll tell you something. Everybody thought you were going to

178

be premature too, fast as your father and I got married. But we fooled them."

"But I could have been?" Margie said confidentially, facing her mother, woman to woman, for the first time.

"You could have been, though I shouldn't admit it to you. Now you run on while I think this through, and don't worry about it. Everything's going to be all right."

"Good-O," Margie said, bouncing off the bed. "You're a good old mom. Hey, look. Allright if I tell Freddy?"

"I don't see why not. It might even help. The sooner he gets used to it, the better."

"Roger," Margie said, bending to kiss her, "Oh, I'm so happy, mommy. You don't know how different I feel. I'm on top of the world."

"I'm glad, dear. And look. About your father. He'll be back. That's why I wanted you to see last night. He's in a meeting now where he's going to learn plenty, and after he's had a chance to think about it, he'll realize where he belongs. He'll be back, baby, and we'll all be together, better than before. He's been sick, but he'll be all right again."

"He had to be," the girl said. "We can't have the wedding without daddy. And you'll be nice to him, mom? You won't let him go away again?"

"I'll be nice to him. So nice he'll think he's in heaven. I'll hug him every morning —"

"Kiss him every night."

"Give him plenty loving and treat him right."

"Because a good man nowadays is hard to find," Margie sang, dancing toward the door. "Bye, mom. You're okay."

The song and her daughter's words were a benison, an assurance somewhere deep inside her that things would truly be all right, and she lay back happily on the empty bed, clutching peace to her like a shroud.

Maybe all this had to happen, she thought, perhaps it was a punishment visited on them for their sins, a scourging from which they would emerge both chastened and redeemed. To have had so much so easily, and to have let it slip away for no reason save their own neglect. But she had learned, she knew that, no matter how painfully and with what ill grace, and now Arthur was undergoing his ordeal by fire. What difference that he'd lose his job at the Henhouse? It bored him anyway, and they had no worries about money. Probably they should move away from Phoenix, escape the world where they had lost themselves, and begin a new life in another country where that wench was dead.

Oh, Arthur, she thought, you think you need that bitch to communicate with? I'm twice as bright as she is, if only you had the sense to see it. And if I'd had the wisdom to let you know.

Maybe even Margie's trouble was a blessing. Sixteen wasn't so young to get married these days, and Freddy Maynard was as good a catch as she was likely to make. Maybe they'd learn from starting so early, even profit from her and Arthur's mistakes, and have the good life the two of them had denied themselves so long. But no longer.

Drowsiness crept over her, and she stretched deliciously. Sleep now. Rest for a little to let the calm take hold, and then she'd call Henry and get herself dressed to be ready for Arthur whenever the time was come. She could wait. Now —

She was almost asleep when the phone rang.

Arthur! She snapped herself awake and grabbed the receiver. "Arthur, darling," she said. "Oh, Henry. How nice of you to call. I was going to call you later on. I . . . of course I do. . . . They *what?* I don't believe it. You're joking . . . You didn't, Henry. You couldn't. Why, you poor man. What's the matter with them? Are they all out of their minds? . . . I might have known. So that's what they were plotting when they were drinking over there last night . . . Yes, of course he was. All evening. Oh, Henry, I can't tell you how sick I am . . . I know . . . Yes, I know. . . . Yes, Henry, I understand how you feel. I'll tell him. . . . No, I don't blame you a bit. I'd feel the same way. . . . Thanks for calling, Henry, and don't you worry. They'll be back to you on their knees after they've had time to think about it. . . . All right, Henry. I'll talk to you later. Goodbye."

She dropped the receiver listlessly in its cradle and fell back on the bed. It couldn't be. It couldn't. It wasn't fair. Goddamn them all. Goddamn him. At the very moment when she was consoling his daughter, abandoned to a problem they should have faced together, defending him to that poor lost child, at that very moment he was conspiring with that bitch and that dissolute Tom Carter to hoodwink the Board into betraying a

180

decent man like Henry Maynard. Jesus, were all men crazy? All of them?

Surely they didn't think they could get away with it. That their innocent act would hold up once she'd told the Board how things really were. She could handle that one all right. In spades.

But Margie. Couldn't it have occurred to Arthur what he might be doing to his daughter when he took out his spite on Henry? Whose dreadful sentence, vindictive and precise, echoed in her mind.

"I want you to tell him something for me, Vicki," he had said, "because I'll never speak to him again. Tell him that if I weren't a godfearing man I'd kill him for what he's done to me. He knew he was guilty, but he didn't hesitate to lie to blacken my reputation. But tell him this too. I'll get even, Vicki, some way I can square with my conscience but that will be just as painful for him, even if it takes the rest of my life. And you'd better tell him you know I mean it, because I do. Do you understand?"

She understood, all right. She could even tell him how, though he'd find out soon enough. Margie would be his weapon, an innocent girl who trusted her father and would, like her mother, be destroyed by him, whose unborn child would give Henry Maynard his revenge. Hell, that lake of the damned which Henry was accustomed regularly to felicitate himself on escaping, could freeze over solid before he would consent to the marriage. An elder of the Presbyterian Church condone wantonness and sin? Trust a jackass like Arthur to give Henry's conscience a field day at the time it would ruin his daughter's life.

Until this morning, Henry would have crawled over ground glass to marry Freddy to Margie. If necessary, he would have wielded the shotgun himself. But not now. Not as long as Arthur Evans was her father. Nevermore.

She brooded, searching, despairing, hating and fearing, returning always to the answer that was no answer until at last, at three by the clock that sat on the table beside her empty glass, she got up and began to dress, readying herself for the thing she had to do.

181

24

The door was open, as she had known it would be. It was
fitting that aping her better's customs would be the bitch's
downfall. Where had the habit started, she wondered as she let
herself in, the tradition of unlocked doors? Out of pride, perhaps, or as a symbol of hospitality, another gallant gesture in a
cause forever lost? No matter. You could case Phoenix's elite by
the doors that were left open all day, and if the fool was determined to act like what she wasn't, she could damned well
take the consequences.

She went quickly upstairs, retracing the steps that had led
to last night's fiasco. The bed was made, a spread masking the
bloody horror she had fled. She resisted the temptation to see if
the sheets had been changed. Time enough for that. First she
must make certain of her ground.

It was as she had remembered it. The bathroom across from
the bed connected with the guestroom opposite. The closet
would accommodate her. Not so wide as a church door, but it
would serve. Adjusting the bathroom doors so that she could
just slip through them, she went downstairs, borrowed a glass,
and found some ice in a tray in the box. From their final drink
the night before, obviously. She didn't have to wonder whose
fingers had touched it last.

Oh, Arthur, Arthur, she thought, a great wave of sadness
overwhelming her, why does it have to be like this, darling, why,
why? It should have been so simple, baby, so easy, all you had to
do was let me love you, have us find together the life we've
both let slip away. Instead of leaving me to act, as always, to
do what is necessary to save the lives that are to come. Your
grandchild, Arthur, whom you would deny.

Now that will do, Vicki, she told herself. The time to be
soupy is over. It's time to act now, time for little Vicki to take
over the show again, and close out the performance now that
she's rewritten the script.

Contempt filled her, and anger, cold and sustaining, as the

memory of last night returned. Did they really think they could do that to her? To Margie? And to all the decent people who tried to make Phoenix a town fit for children to be born in? Thank God she had the sense to see her duty when she had to, and the guts to carry it through. To deal justice where it was due, to the transgressors, and not, like Henry Maynard, to hide behind an innocent child.

She went slowly up to the guestroom, poured herself a drink from the bottle in her handbag, and sat down to wait. Five o'clock. They'd be home in ten minutes, no doubt of that. There'd be no delays this evening. There were rituals to consummate, a triumph to celebrate in a manner befitting the slime in which it had been conceived.

If only she were not so utterly alone. As she had been, she now realized, from the moment of that first phone call, as, on a deeper level, she had been all her life, except for the first happy years of her marriage, before Arthur, for reasons she would now never understand, had closed a door which only too late she had tried to open. Who had ever loved her, really? All they'd wanted was her body, Arthur like the rest of them for all his big words about communion, making such passionate love to her while his mind and heart were with that bitch. Communion was fucking a whore on bloody sheets, descending to a level which decent people should never be forced to see. And which they had a duty to extirpate, a surgical operation like cutting out a cancer to save the body from malignancy and sin.

Well, she had the courage, even if Henry Maynard didn't, and Phoenix, she knew, would thank her for it. What were the strong for, if not to protect the helpless and the weak?

Tires sounded on the gravel. Two cars. They were here.

Unhurriedly, she poured herself another drink, took off her shoes and put them in a corner of the closet, placed her handbag beside them, and sat down again. She felt nothing, she realized with faint surprise, only a calmness, and a certainty now that the time was at hand.

"Ah, baby," Arthur's voice said as the door opened, "damn but it's good to be home."

Home. Anger flared in her, a flame on the ice in her heart.

"Darling, I wish it was," Zelda said. "I wish you could stay with me tonight. I need you. But I know you're right. We have

183

to play it straight, now that we've announced it, until everything is settled and we can really be man and wife. But, God, it kills me to think of me in bed here alone and you in that stupid hotel."

"I'm not gone yet," he said. "Come here."

In the silence that followed, punctuated by urgent whispers before their feet sounded on the stairs, Vicki realized with horror that her hand was trembling uncontrollably, slopping the liquor in her glass until she forced it to her mouth with both hands and drained it. In the panic that overwhelmed her she could not, she knew, take a step from the chair. She sank to her knees and crawled in to the closet, half closing the door behind her as they mounted to Zelda's bedroom.

Stop it, goddamn it, she told herself, gentling the glass into a corner with a palsied hand. Stop it, body. You can't fail me now.

It did no good. Through the sounds of their hasty undressing, her quivering only intensified.

Desperately, she fumbled the catch loose on her bag, worked the cap from the bottle, and, cradling her arms against her breasts, leaned back to let the liquor gush down her throat. The hot whiskey shocked her alive. Fighting to keep it down, gasping in the tiny closet so that she no longer heard the noises in the next room, she realized that the trembling had ceased, and when she could breathe, long shuddering inhalations that she shielded with her hands, her body was again her own.

"Oh, darling," Zelda said out of a silence, "that's enough, baby, enough. Be in me now, lover. I've got to have you now."

A red calm descended on Vicki as the bed creaked. Deliberately, her mind moving steadily as if through a will of its own, she lifted the bottle, took another drink, and placed it carefully in the corner. Snaking into her bag, her fingers wrapped unerringly around the butt of Arthur's thirty-two. She rose effortlessly and inched her way into the bathroom, the pistol firm in her hand.

The beast was on the bed, no longer slumbering or satiate, feeding obscenely on itself. Through the gap in the door she studied it dispassionately. Sweaty and evil, gasping and crooning, a parody of love. The sheets, she noted disinterestedly, were clean.

184

Carefully, bracing the pistol against the door jamb the way her father had taught her, how long ago, on a tree in the woods behind the old house in Spartanburg, she sighted at Arthur's head, squeezed the trigger evenly, and blew his brains into Zelda's face. Crossing quickly to the bed, she looked contemptuously down at eyes blinded by Arthur's gore.

"You silly bitch," she said coldly, placed the gun against Zelda's ear, and fired.

She dropped the pistol into the bloody mess, turned, and walked steadily back to the guestroom. She put on her shoes, picked up her bag, bottle, and glass, and went downstairs. At the refrigerator, she took out the tray Arthur had freed, put three cubes in her glass, and filled it half-full of whiskey, which she drank in one gulp. She placed the bottle and glass neatly beside the sink, went to the phone, and dialed Henry Maynard.

"Henry," she said calmly, "I've just killed Arthur and Zelda. . . . That's what I said. . . . In bed. You'll see when you get here. . . . Zelda's house. I want you to call Chief McCullough for me, Henry, and then come over yourself. . . . Thank you, Henry. I called you first because we're soon going to be family. Margie is pregnant by Freddy, but we can talk about that later. I'll be waiting here, Henry. Please hurry."

Only when she had hung up did the trembling begin, and the horror, so that when Henry Maynard arrived, ten minutes later, he found her standing in a corner, face to the wall, shaking uncontrollably and whimpering like a child.